The Fox and the Phoenix

ERICA LAURIE

The Fox and the Phoenix

Preface

Dear Reader,

The world(s) in this book are fictional, even the one that seems to be our world. Imagine it as you will. The magical worlds are a blending of many world cultures, as our world is filled with much beauty. Regardless of who you meet here during your visit with us, somewhere in the worlds-without-number is someone like you. Perhaps you were once one of the keepers that set the stars in the sky, or maybe you cared for the books in the vast libraries of heaven. Or perhaps, you inhabit one of the many other worlds I spoke of. The possibilities are limitless, after all. You just have to imagine it.

I have tried to be true and consistent with my use of Chinese, which is one of the languages of the nine-tailed fox. Chinese kinship terms can get very complicated, and I've chosen the few I used carefully. Any inconsistencies and mistakes are mine.

Please do not be concerned about how you pronounce the words or the names in this book. As you are reading, the way you *hear* it is the one for you. The only exception is the name Jing'er. It is not Ginger. It is Jing-Er.

I really loved writing this book, and I sincerely hope you'll enjoy reading it.

Sincerely,

Erica

Prologue

The Celestial Empress placed her hand over her husband's and spoke. "He has been alone for many years now. It is not good for him."

The Emperor nodded in thought. "You really care about your foxes."

The Empress laced her fingers through the emperor's and drew him close to her. Her elegant robes were the color of the night sky. Stars glittered upon the fabric as if

they were the very heaven itself. Her dark hair was the color of midnight.

"Have you decided then on who you wish to tie his red string to?" The emperor's robes shone as bright as the sunlight reflected off the moon. The time was night upon the mortal world.

"I have," she said. She held up her palm and a small mirror appeared.

The emperor took the small mirror and gazed upon it. "Ah, one of the hidden ones. This one has an important fate. Is this the best match for them, I wonder?"

"Indeed it is. She alone is a match for him, and he alone can help her survive what is to come."

"See it done then. And watch over them, my dear. Send aid to them should they need it."

The empress smiled and took her thread and needle up, to bind the fate of a nine-tailed fox and a girl who was both of man and fae.

Chapter 1

The fox knew something was wrong the moment he stepped out of the woods. An unfamiliar scent lingered in the air. He frowned and inhaled again. It was a human, that was certain. But why here, at his refuge? Keeping low to the ground, he sniffed and followed his nose right up to his front door. It was ajar. He had left it locked. Locked and warded. Dong looked around. There were decidedly more weeds than on his last visit home.

Maybe his groundskeeper was inside. Dong wondered, however unlikely it was, if he had forgotten the scent of his hired hand.

Dong shifted form, from fox to man, and walked into his front room. A fine layer of dust covered everything. Well, he had come back without contacting his staff to clean up the place. Still, it was not like Mrs. Brown to let things go. It didn't matter. He didn't plan to stay, he was just going to run around the old grounds. He'd uncover what was going on and get his sanctuary back. He'd reset his wards and be on his way.

A noise caught his attention. It sounded like it came from upstairs. He caught that scent again. Dong turned and swiftly climbed the stairs, went down the hallway, and came to a stop at the doorway.

A girl was in the room. A human girl. Her long brown hair was pulled back into a ponytail, and she was making the bed. Dong noticed that the room, and the hallway, had been swept by—what did they call that contraption again—the vacuum. He took a step towards the room and the floor creaked. The girl turned, saw him, and screamed.

"You scared me!" she said, her hand by her heart. He could hear it beating fast. "May I help you?"

Dong took a step back. Could she help him? Help him with what? This was his house, even if he hadn't been there in—how long had it been this time?

"This is my house," he said. "I should be asking you why are you here."

The girl blinked. "Your house? Oh, you must be my landlord. Hi, I'm Riley and I'm your new tenant."

"Te-tenant?"

The girl—no, Riley nodded. "I signed the lease yesterday. I have to thank you for letting me rent a place. As I explained to your leasing agent, I'll get that security deposit in."

Dong was confused. "Leasing agent? Who?"

"Beatrice Ling. I have the papers right here," she said, heading to the desk and pulling out a folder. "I was in such a pickle and really needed a place to crash for a while. My car broke down and—"

Dong cut her off and took the papers. "You can't stay here."

Riley blinked quickly. "What?"

"I don't rent out rooms."

"I... Hey look, it's a legal agreement."

"I do not rent out rooms," Dong repeated.

"I have no place to go if you kick me out," Riley said, staring back into his dark eyes. She had lovely eyes, expressive. He'd need to clamp down on those thoughts and get rid of this interloper.

"That's not my problem," Dong said.

"I'll... I'll sue you for breach of contract!"

She had spunk. Dong tore the paper into pieces. "How?" That should end this.

"You're a jerk," Riley said.

"That may be true," Dong said, pushing his dark hair back from his face. "But you are not staying here." He stepped aside and indicated she could go through the door.

"I'm not leaving," Riley said.

"What did you say?" Dong asked. He had to admit, this girl was intriguing.

"I'm not leaving. Besides, I can't. My car is dead. I will get it towed, soon. I can leave after I get it fixed."

"How are you getting it fixed if you couldn't even afford a security deposit, much less rent?"

"I'll earn some money. Beatrice said I could clean the place up and work for my rent. She also said the housekeeper had recently died, so she'd arrange with the owner about my taking on the job."

Dong drew back. "Mrs. Brown died?" That would explain the dust inside.

"Was that the name of your housekeeper?" Riley asked.

Dong gave a slight nod. "It was."

"I'm sorry for your loss," Riley said. "So, will you let me stay at least until I can get my car fixed?"

Riley was twisting her fingers together.

"But no longer," Dong said. He had no idea why he said it, but for some reason, he felt ... pity.

"And about the housekeeping job?" Riley had hope in her eyes. If one thing his past had taught him was that humans liked to have hope. They worked much better with it.

"That depends on if you can meet my demands."

"Thank you, sir. Um, how should I address you? Beatrice didn't tell me your actual name, she just said 'the lord' and 'fox.' Landlord Fox doesn't seem right now that you are here ..."

"Huli—" He stopped and corrected himself. "Dong Hugh Lee."

"Dong Hugh Lee? Should I call you Mister Lee since you're my landlord and employer?"

He had had many surnames. This was no different, but for some reason, he didn't want her calling him mister. And now he was stuck with the moniker since he'd almost revealed what he was—a huli jing. "It's just Dong."

"Oh," Riley said.

"Well, Miss Riley, how long you can stay on as housekeeper depends on how well you complete your duties."

"Thank you," Riley said.

"Have dinner ready by seven."

"Dinner?"

"Yes. I'll be staying for now and I require food. Until your car is fixed, you may use one of mine to complete your duties."

Chapter 2

Riley stared at the cars in the carriage house. The building itself was dilapidated, but the inside was immaculate. Inside was a row of cars, including a Model T and a 1970s Volkswagen beetle.

"Oh wow," Riley said. "There are some antiques in here. These are all yours?" She walked by them, taking it all in. The man was not only handsome, in his pinstriped suit, wing-tipped shoes, and perfectly styled hair, but he was also well off.

Dong nodded. "Which one do you wish to use?"

Riley rocked on her heels and looked over the vehicles. Well, if she was going to be picking up groceries and running errands she needed a trunk to put things. But she really wanted to drive the lovely green beetle. She cast a longing glance at it before walking back over to Dong.

"You like that one?" Dong said, indicating the green beetle.

"Yeah, I do." Riley chewed her lip and glanced back at the car.

Dong snapped his fingers and keys appeared in his hand. "These are the keys. The car should be fully fueled and ready to go." He waited for her to turn around.

"I can really drive this one?" Riley asked, pulling her eyes from the car long enough to see the keys, which he handed her.

"Yes, but only while you are in my employ. Which will probably be the day after tomorrow. If we're lucky." He checked his pocket watch.

"Why do you say that?" Riley tilted her head and gave him her best *I got this* look.

"Dinner will probably not be good." He frowned. "I'll get your car fixed and then you can drive on out of here and I'll never have to see you again."

"You're such a friendly guy," Riley said. As she climbed into the car she added under her breath, "We'll just see. I bet I can make it so you don't want me to leave and that is when I'll go. Not before. I'm choosing."

Riley pulled out of the carriage house and stopped, rolling down the window. "Hey, where is a grocery store?"

"Beats me," Dong said. "Good luck finding one."

"I'll find it." Riley pulled out her phone and typed *grocery stores near me.* The closest one was about twenty-seven minutes away. She started to pull away when Dong called for her to stop.

"What?"

"You'll need money, won't you?"

"Oh, of course." She should have thought of that.

Dong pulled out his wallet and took out some money, handing it to Riley.

"Thank you," said.

"Don't forget, dinner can not be late even by a minute."

She answered him by waving as she drove off.

Dong walked into his house and went to his room. Over on his desk, a paper appeared, glittering. He strode over and picked it up. It was the lease he had torn to pieces. He lit a candle and burned it this time. He smiled as it turned to dust. Again, it appeared on his desk. He cursed under his breath. This time he took a good look before he took out a vial of sparkly dust and sprinkled it over the paper. As he brushed it off, a royal seal appeared upon it.

"The Celestial Empress," Dong said. He glanced up towards his ceiling and yelled, "I do not let out rooms. I refuse."

Movement caught his attention. A fairy sprite in blue was sitting on his windowsill. "You can't, my lord. Besides, you needed a new housekeeper and Her Majesty has selected one for you this time."

"Is it not enough that I've been punished for my sin? Why torture me?"

"It is really torture having someone living with you?"

The fairy really didn't seem to know, to understand.

"Most assuredly. If one must be stuck living, why must he also have to endure such ..." Dong let his thought trail off. She was young. She was enticing. A tasty morsel of qi if he'd be allowed to—

"Riley is not food," the fairy scolded.

"No, she is not. I am bound to not partake of their energy, their magic, their lives." He felt weary.

The fairy nodded. Dong studied her a moment.

"Are you Beatrice?" Dong asked.

"I am. Beatrice, at your service, my lord. But I can only help three times. This lease was the first."

"Then undo it."

"I am just a messenger. You know that I can not untie fate. But, I can help you twice more." The little fairy turned into a blue songbird.

"I don't need the help of the fae."

The bird spoke once more. "When the time comes, just call for me."

Dong glared at the paper and crinkled it up in his fist.

He may be bound to follow the fate the empress wove for him, but Riley was not. She was mortal. He would just have to make Riley leave of her own free will.

Chapter 3

The Empress walked in her garden, before taking a seat near a small fenced pond. Floating on top of the water were a variety of lotus flowers. Off to the side by itself was a small wilting, nearly black lotus. This lotus was the one that the Empress had placed in her pond when her black-colored fox, the nine-tailed one, had been born. Before it had wilted, the flower had been changing to red. He was falling in love, and with that, changing. When the flower suddenly wilted, the Empress intervened.

Fortunately, the fox hadn't been mortally wounded. However, his heart had been torn asunder. In his grief, he was inconsolable.

"Where's my wife? Where's Jinxia?" he had asked. "I loved her."

"I know. To answer your question, she has gone the way of all those who have died to their next life. She died, so you might live."

"Bring her back to me. Please," he begged.

The Empress shook her head. "What has happened is done. It can not be changed."

Dong's voice broke. "Why? Why did she break the promise we made?"

Jing'er, the female fox, peeked in the room. "Brother, you are well!" She rushed in, happy.

"Get out!" Dong yelled. "You poisoned my wife!"

"She asked me! I had the—"

Dong cut her off. "You didn't have to help her die! Get out."

Jing'er looked at the empress, who nodded. "Dong... I'm sorry. I didn't ..." Jing'er let out a cry and fled the room.

"I'll never forgive her."

"Oh, Dong. Not everything is as simple as it seems. Jing'er is hurting too."

Dong remained silent.

The empress sighed. There was much to tell Dong, about the antidote, Jinxia's motives, and her ultimate choice to save Dong in the end. For now, though, he needed to grieve. The next day, Dong fled back to the mortal realm.

The Empress held up her palm and a small lotus blossom, lacking in color, bloomed. Setting it upon the water, she whispered, "My dear Jing'er. It is time for you to return to the mortal world. Rebuild your relationship with your brother. Help him on his journey. I have faith in you."

Chapter 4

Dinner hadn't gone over well. And it baffled Riley as to why. She knew how to cook spaghetti. Just because the noodles were a little overcooked for *his liking*, that irritating man had merely tasted the food, declared it was trash and left. Not even a word of thanks. Riley blinked back tears.

He wasn't going to make it easy on her, that was certain. But she had no place to go if he truly evicted her. She had

to make this work, at least until she got on her feet. And this was both a place to live and employment.

Idly twirling a strand of red-brown hair, Riley looked out her bedroom window. Tree branches swayed, lightly tapping on her window. Intrigued, Riley went closer. Outside, a black fox ran across the lawn and into the woods.

"Oh wow," Riley said. The only foxes she remembered seeing were at the zoo, and those had been white arctic foxes. She had loved those little guys though. Foxes were special to her. "I wish I could run free like you, little fox," she whispered to the window.

Riley looked at the clock. It was nearing midnight. She yawned. "I should probably get some sleep," she thought. It had been a long day. It had been a rough couple of days. She hadn't let her thoughts return to the events that led to her needing a place to stay. The tears hadn't just been because of Dong's rejection of her food, or that it was clear he was sticking to his plan to kick her out. It was because she *had* been kicked out. Disowned, tossed aside, and abandoned. And it had all started on her eighteenth birthday.

It should have been a happy day. She was turning eighteen. Had turned 18. She had recently graduated from high school and had plans to attend a local community college in the fall. That had always been the plan, she thought.

As always happened, a letter came the day before her birthday for Aunt Pat, the woman who raised her after the death of her parents.

That had changed everything. It included the final check for her support to her aunt. There would be no more. Riley thought this wasn't a problem. She knew she was a financial drain on Aunt Pat because Aunt Pat and her cousin told her so often enough, but surely her part-time job helping Aunt Pat run the noodle shop was enough to make up for that. Her cousin didn't have to work, even part-time. She was a first-year in college and spent most of her time partying. It was unfair, but that was life.

Riley sighed and picked up her pen. She had been lucky to find a place to stay, at least for a time. She'd win that Dong over. After all, not giving up was her motto. Besides, something Beatrice had said resonated with her. Dong had no one, and, if Riley could be his friend, those that cared about him would be grateful. He was very handsome, with his dark hair and brown expressive eyes. It almost made up for his cold behavior. Almost.

She'd do better tomorrow with the food. For breakfast, she'd make scrambled eggs, toast with jam, and a tall glass of apple juice. Maybe for lunch, she'd do trusty peanut butter and jelly. Did Dong like grape, like her, or did he prefer marmalade on his sandwich? She'd need to find out so she could do better with the groceries.

Once Riley finished writing in her diary, she closed it and set her pen down, crawled into bed, and shut off the light. It took a while for her mind to slow down enough to sleep, and before she knew it, it was morning.

Yawning, Riley grabbed her things to shower and headed to the bathroom at the end of the hall. Turning the doorknob, she opened the door and walked in. The room was divided into two parts. One with a vanity, and the second half with the toilet, giant tub, and an independent shower. Bleary-eyed, Riley placed her belongings on the vanity. She'd put her shampoo and conditioner in the shower and start the water before getting undressed. As she turned to enter the second half of the room she crashed into a hard body.

"What?" she said. Did she just crash into the wall? Why was the wall damp? She looked up and realized it was a half-naked man. Dong stood there; a towel wrapped around his waist as he towel-dried his dark hair. Water drops glistened on his surprised, then horrified face. He quickly dropped his hair towel over Riley's head.

"I should be asking you that. Don't you knock first?" Dong asked.

"I'm sorry, but don't you know how to lock the door?"

"I've never locked this one, having had no need. I live alone." He placed his hands on her shoulders and moved her to the side and left the room. He slammed the bathroom door.

Riley pulled the damp towel off her head and turned to look at the door. "Oh my gosh, that was embarrassing," she whispered. Riley set her bottles in the shower, then went and checked the door. It did not have a lock. She sat down on the floor and clutched her racing heart. How was she going to face him now?

It was a worry she didn't need to fret about, for now, anyway. Dong wasn't in the house. He didn't join her for breakfast. He didn't join her for lunch. And he wasn't home for dinner. It was late in the evening when Riley watched a dark little fox run in the direction of the house. A short time after that, the front door opened and closed. Riley left her room and from the banister at the top of the stairs watched Dong walk from the front entry to his library off to the side. It was better to get this over with now. Otherwise, he'd keep avoiding her, wouldn't he? That wasn't a bad thing. If he wasn't there to get annoyed with her, then he couldn't evict her. But then she'd always be on eggshells.

She headed downstairs and went to the kitchen. Rummaging in the cupboard, she pulled out a cup and some tea. She set the water to boil and brewed some tea. Then she carried the hot drink to the library. Knocking tentatively she said, "May I come in? I've made some tea."

"You may enter," Dong said. He was lounging on a chair reading. He didn't look up.

Riley set the tea down. "I'm really sorry about earlier."

Dong gave a nod.

Riley sat down. After a while, she decided the silence was getting to her. What should she say? "You have a lot of books." She felt horrified and thought, *That was stupid. You have a lot of books?!*

Dong grunted.

"I've never seen so many privately owned books." His shelves were wall to wall, and floor to ceiling. *That's not much better*, she thought, *but it is an impressive collection.*

His reply was matter of fact. "When you've lived as long as I have, you have plenty of time to acquire books."

"Mmm. You can't be much older than me," Riley said. She stole a glance at him. She like how he dressed and that he was handsome.

Dong's answer was to turn a page of his book. Riley sighed. He certainly wasn't making this easy.

"I want to be writer," Riley said.

"I thought you wanted to be a housekeeper," Dong replied.

"Not forever. I just need a roof over my head, a job so I can pay for what I need, and a working car so I can attend school next fall."

Dong looked over his book, and their eyes locked for a moment. He cleared his throat and looked down. What he said next came as a surprise. "I'll get a lock for the bathroom in the morning."

Riley's breath caught. "Does this mean I can stay?"

"Perhaps, if you'll leave me in peace so I can read. Run along to your room."

Riley smiled and instinctively wrapped her arms around him. "Thank you!" Blushing, Riley pulled back. "You have no idea how much this means to me."

Chapter 5

Dong watched Riley as she left his library. Did she really have nowhere to go? This home was his sanctuary. And now, he had this troublesome roommate. Why did the Empress want him to take one? And a human at that. One that had a very alluring aura. Her qi would be a feast if he could partake of it. He sighed. Even after all this time, he still craved that energy, that life force. It called to him, teased him, and tortured him. Yet, he had to learn to

let that desire go. Why were spiritual foxes given the desire to take of it if they weren't supposed to? Why was that only an issue in the mortal world? In his birth world, magic was in the air. It surrounded the nine-tailed fox. He breathed it in the air. Here, there were some areas that had magic, but those were fading. It made some things hard. Like, if he used his magic he'd tire out and required rest.

Dong no longer felt like reading. But he'd gone running all day to just avoid the girl. He'd never been in such a state of undress with a woman before. He couldn't get her expression out of his mind. Why did it bother him? It shouldn't have. He used to go to the entertainment house, of all places. Women were plentiful there. He could have had any of them. But he didn't indulge. He'd drink and gamble. He'd break some cups if he got angry. He had slept there on a few occasions. Especially after he lost Jinxia.

His wife. He'd never see her again. They hadn't been truly married, yet. That act hadn't been done. She had been too frail to risk it, especially considering he had yet to learn to control his desire to absorb a human's qi. Dong glanced at his left hand, where he once wore an oath ring. The heart was a strange thing. Until then, he'd only known if he wanted something he hunted it and if he was lucky, claimed it. And he had been a good hunter.

He and his sister Jing'er had both been good hunters. They also discovered that some mortal energy was better than others. Jinxia's had been especially enticing. Very much like this Riley's. Which was why he needed to send Riley away as soon as he could. Before he ... no, that would not happen. He would not lose control, and he would never love another woman again.

Dong was up before dawn the next morning. As was usual, he dressed in a suit. In town, he went to the local hardware store and picked up a new doorknob. His appearance turned quite a few heads. Back at home, he was installing the doorknob when Riley wearily stumbled to the bathroom.

"Good Morning, Dong," she said.

Dong stood up, doorknob with a lock mechanism installed. "The door will now lock."

"I see. Thank you."

Dong noticed that Riley's cheeks were flushed a delicate pink. As she passed him, he inhaled her scent. He closed his eyes and steeled himself. He must not. "I'll leave you to it," he said, indicating the bathroom door.

Riley smiled before slipping through the door. Dong smiled when he heard the door lock.

"Don't forget to wipe down the shower when you are done," he said. "Not a drop can be left behind." A muffled reply came through the door, and Dong's smile grew as he walked away.

One morning, Riley served him pancakes. Dong couldn't find anything wrong with them. In fact, for the past couple of days, he'd been having a harder time finding something to criticize. He decided to pile up on her chores. "The kitchen and bathroom floors need scrubbing. Oh, and the bedding needs to be changed and washed."

By noon, she had everything well underway.

After lunch, he decided to go for a run. He didn't return until much later that night. On the table, she had left his dinner: Fried chicken, mashed potatoes, corn, and rolls. "Riley really went all out," he mused. The same pattern continued for the rest of the week, with Dong adding more and more chores. Riley completed them all. On the seventh day, Riley confronted Dong in his library.

"Have you been pleased with my housekeeping?"

He kept his attention on his book. "You've done well, and I imagine you'll keep getting better."

Riley beamed. "Then is it safe to say I can stay?"

"Is your car back yet?" Dong asked.

Riley shook her head. "The shop said they had to order the part, and it could take another couple of days to get it."

"I see," Dong said, turning a page in his book.

Riley leaned forward. "Is that a yes?"

"Well, you need a job and a place to stay. I need a housekeeper and cook. You've done well with the housekeeping, but your cooking..." He let his voice trail off.

"I can take cooking lessons. And I used to work part-time for my aunt, so I'm really good with noodles. But, would it be possible if you could hire a cook so that I can get a part-time job outside of the house?"

Dong blinked. Why would she need another job? "Why should I do that?"

"It's just that, with you, I'm working for my rent. I'm going to need cash, too. I have to pay my phone bill soon, for one thing. And school is going to cost money."

This left Dong with a dilemma. Did he want her to work outside? Another fox, or worse, might not control himself with how good her life essence smelled. He also, even though he'd not admit it, found that he liked having her around. She cheered up the place.

"I'll make sure to pay you enough. Mrs. Brown didn't live here, so her situation was different, and I honestly hadn't thought much about it."

"How often did Mrs. Brown come?"

Dong thought a moment. "She would come and clean once a week unless I called."

"I'm cleaning every day," Riley said, waving her arms in emphasis.

Dong raised an eyebrow.

Riley held up her hands, almost like a shield. "I'm not complaining. I'm just thinking. Maybe I should get a little more cash than Mrs. Brown did."

"I'll draw up a contract. If you can keep the house clean, make sure to prepare three meals daily, I'll pay fair wages; plus your rent will be covered. However, if the house is ever found in an untidy state, you'll be both fired and evicted."

"Deal," Riley said.

"Then let it begin," Dong said, smiling. Oh, this was going to be interesting. Even fun.

Chapter 6

"**O**ptimism is my talent," Riley said, surveying the large front windows. She held up her fist and set a determined expression. "Fighting!" There were a lot of windows, not to mention the large glass doors leading out the back. Nothing some cleaner, a couple of clean rags, and elbow grease couldn't handle. "Scrub, scrub, scrub," she said as she set to work. It took a while, but finally, she tossed the rag aside and rotated her tired arms.

Wandering into the kitchen, she opened the fridge and grabbed a bottle of cold water. Dong walked in and leaned against the kitchen counter. He smiled, so Riley smiled, greeting him with a nod.

"Did you get the windows finished?" he asked.

"I did."

"That's good. I'll go inspect your work, inside and out." Dong straightened up and turned to leave.

"Outside?" Riley blinked. Surely he didn't expect her to clean all the outside windows, too. A housekeeper worked inside, that's why it was called housekeeping, right?

Dong pressed his lips together with a thoughtful look, then nodded. "There's a ladder in the carriage house."

Riley studied him a moment. Besides the fact that he was always well dressed and somewhat old-fashioned, he had a strange way of talking sometimes. It was almost like he was from a different period of time. She liked his quaint ways. "Why do you call your garage a carriage house?"

"I prefer it."

"I see," Riley said, taking a seat on one of the stools at the counter.

"Don't forget the windows," Dong said, heading out of the kitchen. "I'll inspect them in an hour."

Riley nodded. "Give me a few minutes and I'll get to it."

She finished her water, went to the bathroom, and then headed out to the carriage house. Sure enough, there were several ladders. Since it was a two-story house, Riley opted for the tallest. It took some effort, but she got it to the house and stood it up. Sweat dampened her hair. She should have tied her hair up. It was too late now because if she went inside to her room, she would be too tempted to lie down, and then she'd be in trouble. Her legs and arms were tired after all this work. Grabbing the cleaner and a rag, Riley climbed up the wobbly ladder. The higher she went, the more it wobbled.

"I hate ladders," Riley muttered. She sprayed the window and wiped. One window down. She climbed down, dragged the ladder to the next window, climbed up, sprayed, and wiped. She repeated the process for the next two windows. The library was the next room. Dong was inside, reading. He glanced up as she placed the ladder down. Riley gave him a wave. He turned back to his book, not bothering to respond. Shaking her head, Riley climbed up the ladder. The ground must be not as flat and level here, the ladder was a little more wobbly. Riley reached over and started wiping the window dry. The more she rubbed, the more the ladder wobbled. She clutched the ladder a moment. Once it was steady, she continued to wipe the window. And that was when it happened. A gust of wind blew her hair in her face. Riley dropped the rag and brushed her hair back. Noticing the rag falling she grumbled to herself. A bee buzzed her. Riley swatted it away. The ladder wobbled violently, and she was falling.

In the library, Dong's keen ears heard the ladder wobble, and the plop of the rag hitting the ground. He glanced up and saw the ladder go sideways. Without a second thought, he moved and appeared outside, under Riley. He held up his arms and caught her.

She was staring at him. After a moment, he realized he was still holding her, and set her down. He cursed and asked, "Why were you so careless? Didn't you realize you could break your leg, or knee, falling like that? I can't believe you were—" He stopped when he noticed the slight tremble in her bottom lip and the moisture increasing in her lovely eyes. No, not lovely eyes. Her very ordinary eyes.

"I'm sorry," Riley managed, after a moment.

"Don't let it happen again," Dong ordered.

Riley managed a weak smile. "I won't. I'm usually not that clumsy. Unless I am."

Dong glared at her. She was infuriating. And cute. Which was infuriating and frustrating. He needed a hasty retreat. "I'll put the ladder away. Go make us something to eat."

"Ok," Riley said. "How about garlic parmesan noodles?"

"I don't care," Dong said, grabbing the ladder and heading towards the carriage house. He realized that the ladder probably hadn't been easy for Riley to move, yet she had done it without asking for help. And she hadn't complained. As much as he didn't want to admit it, he admired that. And it had felt good to hold her.

No. It hadn't felt good. It had felt right. Wasn't that the same as good? No, that was better than good. And that was terrifying. He'd have to do something about that. He started by knocking over a flower vase in the entryway. Water spilled on the floor. He knocked over a plant in the library and spread the dirt around. Glancing around, he grabbed books, placing them willy-nilly about. He smiled when came Riley and called him to dinner.

She didn't look pleased.

And somehow, that made Dong feel both happy and... this long unfamiliar feeling. Pain. Something he hadn't felt sense... back then.

Chapter 7

When the doorbell rang, Dong felt relief. "I'll get that," he said.

"I can go—" Riley said.

"Why don't you start straightening in here," he said. He really did not want to stay there, but he couldn't use his ability to get somewhere quickly, not in front of a human. Of *her*.

"Of course," Riley said, giving him a slight bow.

Dong couldn't retreat fast enough. Maybe his plan wasn't good. Maybe, he should try a different way and scare Riley away. But how? He would be banished to the abyss if he harmed her. Humans typically thought of heaven and hell. They didn't know that there were worlds without number in existence. And there were places far worse than a fiery hell. The abyss would eat at you until you ceased to exist. That was far worse.

Opening the door, Dong couldn't believe what—or who— he saw. "Jing'er?" His sister. The very vixen that had once followed him, hunted with him, had supported his desire to be with his wife; and then killed her. Anger filled him, and he shifted form and dove after her.

Jing'er was ready for his attack, as she quickly shifted. The two fought for a while, neither actually biting nor hurting each other. Then Jing'er spoke. "Truce," she said. "Is that how you greet your sister?"

"Since it is you, yes. Why are you here?"

Still in fox form, Jing'er answered, "I've been sent here for a second chance, per the empress."

"You can't stay here," Dong said. What would he do about Riley? Or maybe this was the perfect excuse to send Riley away. After all, Jing'er had been especially fond of dining on human livers. Dong didn't agree on the taste, but it had left fear in the hearts of mortals. Yes, it must be. Surely the empress didn't want to risk a human. Especially one that Dong cared about—to some degree.

Jing'er's ears twitched. Dong heard it at the same time and shifted form. He cursed when he saw Jing'er was still in fox form.

"Dong?" Riley called from the door.

Jing'er gave Dong a wide-eyed look, then smiled.

Dong shoved Jing'er to the side with his foot and the vixen cried. In slow motion, Dong saw Riley rush out the door.

"Oh! A fox. Is it hurt?" Compassion showed in her eyes.

"It?" Dong said. How utterly *it* fit Jing'er.

Riley knelt down and held her hand out to Jing'er. "Oh sweetie, are you hurt? Don't be scared." She turned to Dong. "Can I touch it?"

Jing'er recoiled and growled as Dong yelled, "No!" Placing his hands on Riley, he helped her stand up, turned her towards the house, and whispered, "Go inside, Riley. There is nothing to see out here."

In a stupefied manner, that made Dong feel guilty for some reason, Riley headed towards the house. From there, he knew that she'd return to the library. With a swift movement of his arms, he sent a wave of magical energy into the house, returning the library and the rest of his mess to its former pristine state.

Jing'er laughed as she switched forms. "You haven't been cohabiting have you, brother?"

"What?"

Jing'er watched him. "That slip of a girl. A lover perhaps?"

"Housekeeper," Dong said. He rubbed the back of his neck.

"Then why did it matter that she saw me?"

Dong started walking towards the house. Jing'er followed. He would have to send an inquiry to the empress about his sister. And he needed to figure out how to handle Riley. He couldn't have Jing'er dinning on the girl. For one thing, Riley was his— What was she to him? She was more than energy he wanted. A housekeeper, yes. But more than that, too. She was making him feel things he had thought he put behind him. He had shut everything of his old life away, both the bad and the good. Especially the good when he had finally let his wife go. Riley wasn't a toy to play with. And she was not prey. Was she his friend? He'd have to keep his eye on her and Jing'er for now.

Chapter 8

Riley was standing in the library, staring at the wall of books. Something was different, but she couldn't place her fingers on it. Why had she this feeling she had been doing something in here? There weren't any books out, not even the one that Dong had been reading. There didn't seem to be anything out of place. Perhaps she had been about to vacuum the floor. She turned to head out to grab the vacuum when she collided with Dong again.

She stumbled backwards, and he caught her by the arms and steadied her.

"You really need to watch where you are going," he said tersely.

"I was. You weren't there a second ago. Maybe you need to watch where you are going!" Riley crossed her arms and gave him her best stern stare. Goodness, he had beautiful eyes under his dark hair. And he cut a good figure in his suit.

"Oh," Dong said. "We'll have a guest for a few days."

"We will?" Riley asked. She had to wonder, what was he up to?

"I'll need you to give up your room for now, as it's the guest room. I suppose you can stay in here," he said, looking around the library. Riley said nothing but turned to examine the library. Walls filled with books, a desk with a chair, and another set of chairs with a small table between. This wasn't really a sleeping room.

"Don't you have a spare bedroom?"

"It's not available," Dong said.

"But there's only been—"

"It's not available. There's no bed," Dong said, ending the conversation.

Riley nodded, accepting the way things were turning out. This must be another plot of his to test her abilities. She was going to pass this test. She knew she could pass the cooking one, she just needed to keep at it. And she had passed the cleaning test so far, right? Wait, something was bothering her about that. She had been cleaning. Dong had deliberately made a mess of... of what? She couldn't remember precisely. She looked back into the library.

"I need to get the vacuum," Riley said.

Dong moved out of her way. "Why don't you move your things down here once you've done that. And then, please have dinner available by seven."

"Aye aye, captain," Riley said.

Riley got the vacuum and finished in the library. Then she went upstairs to her room to get her things. Dong had already handed her a thick quilt, to serve as a mattress on the floor, and a pillow. A woman was in her room, doing needlepoint. She was impressive. Both in beauty and skill.

"Wow, you're good at that," Riley said.

Jing'er smiled. "I've been doing it for a long time. Very long time." She stuck the needle in the fabric and pulled it through.

"I'm Riley," Riley said.

"Jing'er," the eerily beautiful woman said. She had similar features to Dong. Were they related? As if she could read her mind, the woman said, "Dong is my brother."

"I'm glad he has family," Riley said.

Jing'er raised an eyebrow. "Why is that?"

"Family is important," Riley said. "Or, it should be."

Jing'er seemed to mull that over. "Where is your family, Riley?"

"My parents died when I was little. I have—had an aunt who took me in for a while."

"Ah," Jing'er said. "Some people value their family."

"Don't you and Dong?" Riley said.

"Sometimes," Jing'er said. "We had a falling out once. But that was long ago. I'm here now to amend for that."

"I think that's admirable. You got this." Riley held up her fist in encouragement.

Jing'er merely nodded and went back to her needlework. "I put your items back into the box I found. I hope you don't mind that I'm displacing you."

"Not at all," Riley said. "I'll just take this then and leave you to your work. Oh, and it's nice to meet you."

Jing'er looked up. "It's nice to meet me?"

Riley smiled. "Yes. I hope we can be friends."

"Friends," Jing'er said. "Friends... I don't know how."

"That's okay," Riley said. "It's really simple, you'll see."

Riley was happy as she made her way to the library. For dinner, she fried up some chicken. For sides, she made some fries, rolls, and fresh veggies. For dessert, she even made an apple pie. A good old-fashioned family dinner was perfect for Dong and Jing'er reuniting. Wasn't it grand that they were willing to let the past go for the sake of family love?

Dinner started off awkward. When Riley sat down to join them, Jing'er looked askance at her. Riley gave a questioning look, wondering if she had anything on her face.

"Jing'er said, addressing Dong in the term for an older brother. "You let your hired help dine at the table with you nowadays?"

Dong gave no outward reaction. "No, that would be improper."

Jing'er tilted her head towards Riley.

Dong's answer was to reach for the plate of chicken. He placed the drumstick on Riley's plate.

Jing'er smiled. "It's good that you still remember."

Dong looked at Riley. "Once you have filled your plate, please dine in the kitchen."

"Oh," Riley said. "Ok." Heart pounding uncomfortably, Riley finished filling her plate and went into the kitchen.

"That was rude," she heard Jing'er say.

Riley didn't hear Dong's reply because she walked right out of the kitchen through the back door. She wasn't sure how long she could hold back the tears. Hadn't she just made friends with Jing'er? All week, Dong had let her dine at the table with him. It had made her feel she belonged in some small way. Why was she just a hired hand now? She took a few deep breaths. She had no desire to let him see her weakness. It wasn't that Dong had snubbed her, right? It was because she was just overwhelmed from being disowned and not having a family. That's why she had started to think of Dong as family.

Yes, that had to be it.

Chapter 9

After dinner, Riley didn't talk to Dong. She simply gathered the dishes up and retreated back to the kitchen. He sat at the table, listening to the water run and to the sound of dishes being washed. He thought back to dinner. He knew Riley well enough now to feel confident that she'd been unhappy when he sent her to the kitchen to eat. Maybe allowing her to dine at the table with him had been a mistake, because now she expected to eat with

the family. If he and Jing'er could still be considered family. And since he intended to send Riley away, he needed to set some boundaries in their relationship. That would make it easier, wouldn't it?

He touched the table and a sheet of paper and a pen appeared. He normally did not like using magic here in the mortal world. It aged you, leaving you tired and old unless you obtained energy from somewhere. The best source of renewal was human energy. Then it was animals, and finally plants. He had promised his empress that he would endure it and not consume human energy if he would be allowed to stay. In his birth world, magic flowed freely, so he didn't need to replenish it in the same way. Here, you were always hungry for it. And Riley didn't make that easy for him. Because of this, he needed permission to send her away. He'd find her an apartment and set her up. Surely the empress would agree to that. After all, Jing'er had somehow lived. Was he grateful for that? They were immortal after all. Dong picked up the pen and began writing. Once finished, he folded it and sent it flying, where there was flash of light and it vanished.

He needed to hunt. He'd been using magic quite often as of late. First, to catch Riley when she fell off that ladder. He'd used it to get to her before she hit the ground. He could feel the memory of her landing in his arms, her surprised look. He had stared a moment. Besides being alluring because of her inner energy, she was pretty. It had taken everything he had to not devour her at that moment. Or kiss her. He wasn't sure which. So he berated her for being clumsy. The second time was to clean up the disaster he had created when Jing'er had shown up and foiled his plans.

He had decided to use his sister to oust Riley. He gave Riley's room to Jing'er. He didn't have to do that, he had a spare bedroom. It was currently a storage room that contained items from his long life. The basement was his workout room, which he'd use more when the cold winter came. It was still pleasant enough outside where he preferred to run in the woods.

Dong stretched. It was time to go for a run. Perhaps he would find some small game on his hunt. Mice or some birds. His lips twitched into a smile when he pictured an annoying bluebird. It wasn't really a bird though, it was a fairy. Beatrice. He'd be careful and not catch any songbirds. He needed something larger though. Maybe a quail or two.

He loved running, feeling the wind against his dark fur. Mortal eyes usually didn't see his nine tails, unless they believed in magic. As time had gone on, the belief in magic died down. People even didn't remember the celestial royal family. They had a vague concept about a god, and sometimes multiple gods. They also didn't recall the great dragon that guarded the world, locking away his own brother in prison when he had tried to destroy the world.

This forgetting was good for those magical creatures that stayed in the mortal realm. There were a few foxes like him. They usually stuck to the mountains in faraway lands in the east. Fairies could be found scattered about the world. The rest of the fae—or the elves, goblins, and others— usually stayed in the realms of magic. This is the knowledge that Dong knew.

He ran to the trees and looked back. He could see a figure in the library window. Riley. He shook his head and ran into the woods. He was grateful his home had these woods. When he first came here, it didn't. He had planted the trees and then waited patiently for them to grow. He avoided the town as much as he could as it built up. When he couldn't, he tended to use a little magic to have any memory of him fade. His existence was a rumor, a passing thought. He also encouraged people to feel afraid of his house and grounds, so that they avoided it. It had worked quite well. Until Riley had moved in. It hadn't worked on her.

His thoughts kept returning to that woman. What was he going to do? Well, first off, he needed to find some small game. He sniffed the air and the ground. Dusk was a good time to hunt, and his favorite time.

He didn't know how long he hunted. Every time he thought of Riley, he had pushed himself further. It was growing late. He was tired. Also, there was a hint of rain in the air, so he should return home. As he turned towards home, thunder rumbled in the distance. Getting stuck out in the storm was not appealing. He paused and glanced around, checking to make sure no one was nearby before he picked up his speed. He was home a few minutes later.

Thunder boomed and the eerie glow of lightning lit up the room. Riley's heart pounded, the ache in her chest both from the drum of her heart, and the growing fear. She hated storms. Had hated them since that day. She counted the seconds from flash of lightning to thunder. She got to ten before it flashed again. Two miles. Rain pounded against the window, and upon the roof. She huddled under her blanket, blinking back tears. "One Mississippi, two Mississippi, three Mississippi, four Mississippi, five Mississippi, six—" When the boom came, she shrieked. Not even a mile away. The sound of rain increased, and the lightning was multiple. "Stop, please, stop," she begged. The loudest thunder yet raged on. Riley was in full panic.

"It's okay," Dong's voice said, in the dark. His arms pulled her to him. "Are you afraid of storms?"

"Yes," Riley whispered, tears running down her cheeks. A thumb gently brushed them away.

"You are safe," Dong said. "I won't let anything happen to you."

Riley wrapped her arms around him and sobbed. When the lights and booms of the storm raged, she clutched him tighter, but she didn't scream. After a while, the storm started to fade, and she fell asleep.

Carefully, Dong eased her down and tucked her in, his shirt damp from her tears.

Dong was unable to sleep after holding Riley, so he opted to make breakfast. Riley entered the kitchen as he finished scrambling the eggs. The toaster popped. "Can you get that?" he asked.

Riley nodded and reached for the toast. She spread butter and jelly on the slices, then placed them on the plate with the rest of the loaf already toasted. "You've been busy."

Dong looked up. "Uh, yeah."

"Have I not been making enough toast in the morning?" She smiled. "I can toast you know."

Was she teasing him? Unsure of what to reply, Dong picked up a slice and popped it into her mouth. "No questions." He let go of the bread.

Riley chewed and swallowed, holding the bread to keep it from falling. "I'll help by setting the table." She pulled out three plates. She set hers on the kitchen table and took the other two to the dining room.

"Riley," he called.

Riley turned back. "What?"

"Set your plate out there too. You eat at the main table."

"But Jing'er—"

"My house, my rules. If Jing'er doesn't want to eat with the help, she can eat in the kitchen."

Riley smiled, and Dong's heart did a strange thud and he smiled back.

Chapter 10

Riley walked into the library where Dong was sitting in his comfortable chair reading. "The car shop called. My car is ready to be picked up."

"I'll take you to get it then," Dong said, his heart dropping. She could leave now. His time with her was coming to an end.

"Thank you," Riley said.

"I'd like to come," Jing'er said. She was doing needlepoint by the window.

Riley frowned. It was fleeting, but Dong noticed it. His heart warmed at the possibility that Riley wanted just his company.

"It's only picking up a car," Dong said.

"I can tell when I'm not wanted," Jing'er said.

Riley was quick to assure her. "No, you can come if you want."

Now it was Dong's turn to frown.

"Perfect. I wanted to see what the town my brother has chosen to call home is like."

"There's not much to see," Dong said. "Which is why I picked it."

"I'm sure you have had much to do with its lack of growth," Jing'er said. She stood up and patted her hair. "I'll go freshen up." She practically skipped from the room.

"Make it quick," Dong said. He set his book down.

"Is that a good book?" Riley asked.

"It has its moments," Dong said.

She walked over to one of the shelves and ran her fingers along a few books. "Maybe one day, my books will join your shelves."

Dong blinked. He envisioned some worn romance novels joining his well-cared-for collection before he remembered. Riley had told him she wanted to be a writer. "There's nothing stopping you from writing."

She turned to face him. "Everybody told me that writing won't pay the bills. That I need to get my head out of the clouds."

"Your head was in the clouds?" He pointed up towards the sky.

Riley laughed. "You know what I mean."

"I might not," Dong said. "I don't see why you can't be a writer. Hu—life is short, you should go for it."

Riley beamed at him. Again with the erratic thumping in his chest.

"Thank you, Dong. So, how about it?"

"How about what?" Dong could hear Jing'er approaching, so he stood up and straightened his suit coat.

"About my book being on your shelf." Riley's eyes were watching him.

He almost said no, just out of habit. But, somehow he realized he really wanted to know what she'd write. "Write it first, then I'll let you know."

Jing'er stood by the passenger door as if waiting for Dong to open the door for her. Instead, he nodded his head towards the back. Jing'er looked shocked but regained her composure. "The hired help rides in the front?" She spoke low enough so only he heard her.

Dong glared. Riley was not just hired help.

Jing'er smiled. "I was given a crash course on what I've missed in the mor—"

"Jing'er," Dong growled.

"Never mind," Jing'er said.

Dong opened the passenger side door for Riley. She climbed in and snapped on her buckle.

"So," Riley said, as Dong walked in front of the car and over to the driver's side. "What was Dong like as a kid?

"He was a good *kit,*" Jing'er said. When Dong gave a low growl, she laughed. "Kid," she corrected. "He followed me around a lot, doing the usual annoying brother bit. But, I would do most anything for him too."

"I wish I had a sibling. I envy you." Riley said.

"Why is that? A man's life may be short in the scheme of things, but you get to love more deeply and more passionately than others. It's what powers your energy so well. For us, it is different. It's why so many want to be hum—."

Dong coughed. He turned the ignition and pulled away from the house.

"I've said too much," Jing'er said.

"I think I understand though," Riley said. "Life is short. And there's much power in love. I like to believe love can conquer all. Like in the fairy tales. Maybe someday my prince will find my missing glass slipper and I'll get to try it on, and then he'll take me away to his castle." Riley looked out the window.

"You have glass shoes?" Jing'er asked.

Riley laughed. "No, it's a reference to a story called Cinderella. Don't you know it?"

"No," Jing'er said.

"Like me, both her parents died and she had to live with her wicked stepmother and two ugly stepsisters. Only, I had a wicked aunt and a gorgeous cousin."

"Shouldn't it be ugly cousin?" Dong asked.

"Not in this case," Riley said. "She was beautiful, and she knew it."

"I can take care of that," Jing'er said.

"Jing'er," Dong said.

Jing'er threw up her hands, "I was joking.

"Always the trickster," Dong said. "Tell us the story, Riley."

And so Riley told the story, about a girl and a glass slipper given to her by her fairy godmother.

Dong pulled into the car shop, parked, and got out of the car. Riley had just placed her hand on the latch when Dong opened it for her.

"Ah, playing the perfect gentleman, brother?" Jing'er said as Riley climbed out.

"You stay here," Dong told Jing'er, before following Riley into the shop.

Chapter 11

The Empress sat next to a large round window that overlooked a beautiful, white-flowered willow tree. The white blossoms would give way to a special fruit in a few hundred years. She opened a letter and read it again. What was she to do about her beloved fox Dong? She sighed and tapped her hand with the paper.

The emperor took notice and asked, "What is it, my dear?"

"My little fox is troubled. Do you remember the trouble he and his sister caused in the mortal world?"

"Which trouble are you speaking of?" The emperor took a seat next to his wife and clasped her hand in his. "Some of your foxes are always getting into trouble, being mischievous. This pair was particularly good at it." He was teasing, and the empress knew.

"He fears for the girl," the empress said, turning her concerned gaze to her white-haired husband. Despite the white hair, he still looked as youthful as the day they married. It had been the day he had ascended the throne, at the behest of the great dragon.

"Oh?" The emperor looked pleased and stroked his beard. "He is growing up."

"It does appear so. He wants permission to send her away."

"Why don't you grant him this? Is not the point of the red string to help guide them together?"

The empress sighed again and looked away, once again looking at the blossoms. "It is not good to be alone," she said. "He's been alone for a long time."

"What is his reason to send the girl away?" the emperor asked.

"He is afraid he will harm her and drain her life away."

"That is a very real possibility, is it not?" He gently squeezed his wife's hand.

The empress placed her other hand atop her husband's comforting one. "I suppose. But you've said it yourself. He's grown up."

never been so messy while cooking bread. She had also never been as cute with a smudge of flour. Dong had the sudden urge to wipe the flour off Riley's cheek. Instead, he spoke.

"I have returned home. Please have my dinner ready and brought up to my room. Immediately," he added.

Riley turned her gaze to him and locked eyes. "You're back."

"I am."

"I'm making bread right now," Riley said. "I'll bring you something to eat as soon as I get this kneaded." She turned back to the dough and resumed kneading it, putting greater effort behind it.

Dong walked to the stairs and took them two at a time, heading up to his room. He gathered his things for a shower. After showering, he returned to his room and sat in his chair. Maybe he should read while he waited for Riley to bring him food. He looked at his book. He looked at his watch. Riley should have dinner ready for him soon. He heard footsteps approaching. Good, she was coming. A knock on his door had him focusing on his book. He cleared his throat. "Come in!"

Riley entered with a tray. On it was ... what was that? It looked like two pieces of bread with something between each slice. He inhaled. Was that peanut butter and jelly?

"I wasn't expecting you," Riley said, setting the tray down on the end table he was sitting by. "I hope you don't mind the sandwich."

He held up a hand. "It's fine." He set the book down. What should he say? Oh, he had it. "How have you been?"

Riley raised an eyebrow.

He tried again. "Jing'er has been good?"

"Yes," Riley said. "If that will be all, I'll get going." Riley turned to leave.

"Wait," Dong said, nearly standing up.

Riley turned to face him.

"Uh," Dong said. He needed to think of something to say. He didn't want Riley to leave yet. "My bedding needs to be changed."

"I'll get right on it," Riley said, leaving. Moments later she was back with fresh bedding. She stripped the bed, replacing all the linens.

Dong watched, wondering what else to say. It took him a moment to realize that Riley was talking to him, her arms filled with sheets. What had she said? Oh, she was bidding him a good night. Was she not planning on seeing him the rest of the evening? Before he realized what happened, Riley had left the room. He turned his attention to the sandwich. He picked up a half and took a bite.

That hadn't gone at all like he had wanted.

How exactly had he hoped returning home would go? That Riley would greet him with open arms? He smiled, imagining it. Pretty Riley, with her flour smudges giving him a hug as he walked into the kitchen. Or he'd wrap his arms around her from behind, kissing the top of her head. She'd turn to him with a smile. Later, they'd eat warm bread, dipped in butter and honey. He shook his head. No.

That wouldn't do. He wasn't falling for Riley. He would never love again.

He finished his sandwich. He could smell the fresh-baked bread. Maybe Riley would bring him some. He heard the front door open and close, followed by talking. Jing'er had returned. Maybe he could talk to Jing'er about Riley. He and Jing'er had been close once. He took up his plate and cup and headed for the kitchen. He paused just outside the kitchen. The women were talking.

"Dong is back," Jing'er said. It wasn't a question.

"Yes," Riley said. "He asked for dinner in his room."

"Whatever for?" Jing'er said.

At the same time, the women said, "Do you think he's avoiding me?" Then, "Why would he be avoiding you?"

"Fetch me some wine," Jing'er said.

"Of course," Riley said. Dong heard her grab glasses—no, a single class. Riley wasn't going to drink. The wine cabinet opened.

"I'll pour," Jing'er said. "It's a long story. Where should I start?"

Dong's heart started pounding. What should he do? Should he stop them? He was about to when a blast of cold hit him. A small dragon hovered by him, reached out and grabbed his shoulder. He felt a deep chill and then he appeared in the heavenly palace's garden. The dragon released him as he saw the empress. He set his plate and cup down, and immediately bowed low.

"You may rise," the empress said. "Walk with me."

Dong rose and fell into step with the empress.

"You worry about her," the empress said.

"I do," Dong said. "I—." He suddenly stopped and held up his hand. A faint red string was attached to his little finger. "What's this?"

The empress smiled and turned back to face Dong. "You were destined to meet Riley and she you. What will you do with that knowledge?"

"Riley needs to be far away from me. From Jing'er." Dong's face paled. "And she's *alone* talking with Jing'er right now."

The empress was calm and soothing. "Jing'er knows not to reveal what you both are. It is up to you to tell Riley, if you choose to."

"I have not forgiven Jing'er," Dong said.

The empress shook her head. "Oh, Dong. Forgiveness is a great gift to give yourself."

"I felt pain," Dong said.

"As you should have," the empress said. "I would be worried had you not felt pain."

"I don't understand," Dong said.

"Someday you will." The empress nodded to the dragon. "It is time."

"Wait," Dong said. "What about Riley?"

"Riley's destiny is in her hands. Only she can untie what has been done."

"What does that mean?" Dong asked.

"You will know when the time is right. Until we meet again," the empress said, as the dragon touched Dong's shoulder. In the blink of an eye, Dong was back at home. His plate and cup were back in his hands. The cold between realms had frozen his fingers and he dropped them. The sound of shattering glass announced his presence.

"Why is it so cold?" Riley said, coming over to Dong. She reached out and touched Dong's hands. "Are you okay? You're freezing!" She took moment to inspect him. Her expression was worried. "Let me clean this up," she said of the glass.

"I got it," Dong said. He gently touched Riley's face. "Sleep," he whispered. Riley fell asleep as Dong gathered her into his arms. He made a swift flick of his hand, and the broken glass flew into the trash.

Chapter 13

Riley awoke to early morning sunshine pouring in the window. When did she go to bed? She didn't remember that. She sat up. Where was she? This wasn't the library. She looked around carefully, then gasped. She was in Dong's room. Not only that, she was in his bed. Oh no! What had happened?

She jumped out of bed, which was thankfully empty of the man. In fact, it looked like the only disturbed bedding

was where she had been resting. A knock sounded at the door and Jing'er walked in.

"Good morning, Riley," Jing'er said. "I've brought your clothing."

"Where's Dong?" Riley asked.

Jing'er shrugged. "He went for a run after he carried you up here. Do you remember anything?"

Riley shook her head. "I remember you and I were in the kitchen. Then ... broken dishes. After that, nothing." Riley frowned. "And it was oddly cold in the kitchen. Wait, what happened to the bread I was baking?"

"Dong got the loaf out of the oven for you," Jing'er said. "He seems to like doing domestic things now." She laughed. "Go take a shower. My brother wanted to take you somewhere today, so you best get ready."

"But—"

"No buts," Jing'er said.

Riley took her clothing from Jing'er and made her way to the bathroom. She was so confused. Why had she fallen asleep? As she washed her hair, she kept running through things in her mind. Dong had dropped his dishes. Yes, that had happened. The air around him was cold. Perhaps that was due to the kitchen being hot from baking bread. Dong had touched her cheek, cradling her face in his hand when he had whispered to her. What had he said? Sleep.

And then she woke up in his bed? She must have been tired, to have collapsed like that asleep. How embarrassing.

After her shower, Riley went into the kitchen and poured herself some cereal. As she was eating, Jing'er walked into the room. "Dong's in the library and he'd like to talk to you."

"Ok," Riley said. She set her bowl down and went to the library. "You wanted to see me?"

Dong looked up. "Yes. My bedding," he said, nodding towards the floor, "will need to be washed and put away."

"You slept in here?" Riley asked.

"Of course, why do you ask?"

Riley's face flushed red. "Well…"

Dong cleared his throat. "I needed to work late last night, that's why I let you make use of my room."

"So that must be why you had me change your bedding earlier," Riley said, trying to piece everything together.

"Uh, yeah." Dong shrugged, flipping through some papers on his desk.

"I'm sorry, I must have been really tired," Riley said.

"I've been working you too hard," Dong said. "It is my fault."

"Jing'er said you had something to show me today?"

Dong smiled. It was both inviting and … was creepy the word she wanted to use?

"I do," he said.

Riley wasn't sure if she should be excited or alarmed. Maybe both.

Chapter 14

Dong had thought about it for quite some time. Perhaps the best way to get Riley to leave was to reveal what he was. And that would mean telling her about Jinxia. He'd tell Riley everything. She would then leave, obviously. He was a nine-tailed fox. They killed people and ate their livers. He could kill *her*. He'd caused his wife's death. While it was true he hadn't forgiven Jing'er for giving Jinxia the poison, it was he that caused Jinxia to drink

it. If he had been a normal man, things would have been different. If he wasn't careful, he would harm Riley.

He waited patiently for Riley to start the laundry. Why had he given Riley his room anyway? He could have conjured up a comfortable bed for her in the library if he hadn't wanted to put her on the floor. He didn't need to do it the human way. But he had, all the same.

He was losing it. Well, by that evening Riley would jump in her car and flee. He'd give her severance money. How much was reasonable? He had no idea. She could live quite comfortably if she'd let him arrange it.

Riley was dressed in jeans and a green t-shirt with a sweater when she hopped on over to where he was outside. She seemed happy.

"Where are we going?" she asked

"One of my favorite places. But first, I need you to turn around. I'm going to blindfold you."

Riley raised an eyebrow but complied. Dong tied the blindfold. "Can you see anything?" he asked.

"Nothing," Riley said. "Is this really necessary?"

"It is," Dong said. "I want you to pay attention. Don't trust your eyes. Just feel. Remember how cold it was by me before you fainted?"

"I fainted?"

"I may have helped," Dong admitted. "But never mind that." Dong took Riley's hands and positioned himself so she could climb into his back. "Riley," he said. "Lean on my back."

"You're giving me a piggyback ride?"

"It's the easiest way for me to take us to where we are going," Dong said from his crouched position

"Which is?"

He felt impatient. "Climb on."

Riley did as he asked.

He focused on her arms around his shoulders and neck, her weight on his back. Her closeness was comforting. He reminded himself that this was for the best. It was the best way to protect her.

"Hold on tight, we are going to travel fast." He ran, using his speed.

Riley gasped. "Did you get on a bike without me realizing it?"

Dong laughed. "Do you think I did?"

Riley shook her head. "No. That would be impossible."

Dong ran through the trees. He could run fast, either as a human or a fox. He preferred to run as a fox. He came to a stop, deep in the woods. "What if I told you, I am impossible?"

"I don't know. How would you be impossible?" Her voice trembled a little. She was worried. This was good. Right? It's what he wanted.

Dong said nothing as he waved his arms in an intricate pattern—one that would open the portal to his world. His former home. The portal shimmered into view and he took them through it. It was already winter here, this close to the mountains.

"It's cold," Riley said.

"It is winter where I come from," Dong said, removing the blindfold.

Riley looked around. Snow covered the landscape. The sky was dark, stars twinkled. So many stars. "It's beautiful," Riley said. "I don't think we are in Kansas anymore."

"We weren't in Kansas," Dong said.

"Haven't you seen the Wizard of Oz?"

"Oh. Then yes, we are not in Kansas anymore, Dorothy."

"Do I get to wear ruby slippers?" Riley lifted a foot and wiggled her foot around. She wore sneakers.

"I had forgotten it would be winter," Dong said. "I didn't have you dress properly." With a wave of his hand, he fixed that. Riley was outfitted into a warm coat and sparkling red boots. "Your ruby slippers," Dong said.

"Am I dreaming?" Riley blinked, then pinched her arm. "Ouch! No, I don't think I am dreaming." There was a bit of awe in her voice.

"There's one more thing," Dong said.

Riley nodded, waiting.

Dong shifted form, becoming a black fox with tails. Nine to be exact.

Riley gasped and stepped back. It was more of a scream. After what seemed almost unbearably long to Dong, she asked, "What are you?"

"I'm a fox," Dong said. "I can shift forms."

She took a step closer. "You have nine tails!"

"Yes." Each question felt like a stab in the heart. He had to go on.

"Foxes only have one tail," Riley said, an unasked question lingering between them.

"I'm a magical fox. We are immortal."

"Is Jing'er a fox?" Riley asked.

"Yes," Dong said.

"I remember now. She was the one that you were talking to outside."

Dong was startled. "You remember?" How did she remember? He had bid her not to remember. Mortals could be easily influenced by his mind magic. It was why Jinxia's father had opposed their match. He had claimed there was no way to know if Jinxia really loved him. As if he would do something that dishonorable!

"Oh my gosh! You are soo adorable," Riley said, kneeling down and wrapping her arms around his neck. Dong tried to pull away. But he was only a fox at the moment. At least, that is what he told himself.

In truth, he wanted her to hold onto him. At least, for a moment.

Chapter 15

"Riley, you are choking me," Dong finally managed to say.

"Oh, I'm sorry." Riley pulled away, putting her hands together as a delicate pink blossomed on her cheeks.

"You aren't frightened?" Dong asked.

"No," Riley said. "It is, actually, curiously comforting."

"What do you know of the nine-tailed fox?" Dong asked, ignoring her last statement. How was it comforting he was a fox?

"Nothing, actually," Riley said. "You can't be worse than a vampire though."

"What do you mean?" Dong wasn't sure where Riley was going with this.

"Vampires are creatures of the night. They prey on humans and drink their blood." Riley clutched her neck and made gurgling sounds. "Foxes are little puppies. So how can you be that bad?"

"What if I were to tell you that we're more like werewolves?"

Riley chewed her bottom lip, which brought Dong's attention to them. Were they as soft as they looked? He started to lick his lips before he shook his head, suddenly irritated. His goal tonight was to get Riley to willingly leave. That is what the empress must mean. The empress had brought them together, and only Riley could undo it by leaving. Dong had to follow what the empress commanded. Riley did not. Riley had her free agency. Dong was a fox. An animal. He wasn't worthy to be with Riley.

"I doubt that," Riley said.

"Oh?"

Riley nodded. "For one thing, you haven't changed during the full moon."

"How do you know? Perhaps I had left the house."

Riley waved her arm as she talked. "You change at your will, by your will. Werewolves have no control. Unless we're talking Twilight wolves here."

"I don't follow," Dong said.

Riley put her arm around Dong's furry shoulders. He tried to shake her off, but it didn't work. He needed his arms. He changed forms, picked up her arm, and cast it aside as she talked.

"I think you need to read the books. Much better than the movies," Riley said. "But what I meant is, in those books, Jacob's tribe could change form at will, although the first shift was involuntary and related to the vampires being nearby."

"I was a fox before I could take the human form," Dong said.

"What's it like, being a nine-tailed fox?" Riley looked at him.

"Lonely," Dong said. He instantly regretted it, as Riley placed her small hand on his larger one and gave him a gentle squeeze.

"I know lonely. You don't have to be alone, you know. I'm here."

Dong realized she meant it. "Riley, you aren't getting it." Dong stood up and walked a few steps away, before turning back to look at her. "I could easily kill you."

"You won't. I trust you,' Riley said.

Dong shifted his form, knocking Riley down to the ground, a fox once again. "You shouldn't."

Her answer was to hug him again. "You won't hurt me," Riley said. She buried her face in his fur.

"I killed my wife," he said.

Riley drew back. Dong didn't like her pulling away. But this was for her own good. He decided to shift to part human, part fox. He had fox ears and fox tails as he related his story.

His voice was barely more than a whisper. "That's right, I caused the death of my wife."

"What happened? Was she a fox too?" Empathy was in Riley's eyes.

Dong drew in a deep breath. "It happened many years ago. Over two hundred to be exact. Jing'er and I were living grand at the time. The people had nearly forgotten the nine-tailed fox, so it was a prime hunting ground. We would hunt at night, seeking those that committed crimes. We could replenish our magic by dining on the energy of humans more quickly than other living things. Jing'er especially appreciated how it worked like the fountain of youth. Using our magic in your world, weakens and ages us. Death is a very real possibility."

"Didn't you say you are immortal?"

"Yes, but so is the human soul. Your body simply isn't. After this life, your spirit will go on living in the next. We foxes are spirit animals."

Riley reached out and placed a hand on Dong's arm. "You feel normal to me."

Dong let out a hard laugh. "Death is different for us. Some say we cease to exist. Others say we will reincarnate as a human if we are deserving, or as a mortal fox if we are not. If we ask one of the gods, they say we'll know when the time is right."

Dong grew silent for a while.

"Tell me more about your wife."

"Her name was Jinxia. She was the most beautiful creature I had seen. She wasn't afraid of me, of what I was. Her father opposed our marriage, but she insisted. He relented and a date was set. However, she was frail and we could not yet risk a physical union. Instead, I claimed her as mine by bonding us with an oath ring. My oath was to protect her, and if I lost control and killed her, I would die with her."

"Surely you are being overly dramatic."

Dong sighed. "I wish I was. There are reasons behind the stories about a nine-tailed fox killing her bridegroom on their wedding night. What if I too, devoured my wife, leaving nothing but a lifeless corpse?"

Riley shivered. "I don't like the way you said that."

Silence stretched on for a few seconds, or eternity, Dong wasn't sure which. Was she scared? Was she understanding why he was dangerous and why she had to leave?

"What's it like?" Riley said, inching a little closer.

"What's what like?" he asked.

"Devouring energy?" she answered.

"Why do you ask?" Dong said. He wasn't sure where she was going with this. She was so close he could feel her breath.

"Will you try absorbing mine?"

Dong shot several feet away. "No." What kind of question was that?

"Why?" Riley asked.

"I don't think I could stop," Dong said softly.

"But you could, right?" Riley said. She had total trust in her eyes.

Dong gazed at Riley. She was so unexpected. Her life energy was perfect for him. Even more so than Jinxia's had been. The perfect balm for his soul. The one that if he started to pull it in, he'd devour her whole. And nothing could stop him. Perhaps not even her death. And he couldn't allow that. Ever. He loved her, and he realized, that was why her qi called to him so. It was her very essence, her soul. He gave no answer as Riley stood up, her legs trembling. From nerves or the cold, Dong wasn't sure.

Riley looked at him. "Well, as interesting as this has been, I'm ready to wake up."

His heart panged him painfully. But this had to be done. "You are very much awake," Dong said.

Riley clicked her heels together three times and closed her eyes. "There's no place like home."

Dong barked a laugh. "Are you scared yet?"

Her eyes flew open. "Of you, no." She squared her shoulders and smiled at him.

She was trying to lighten the mood, he realized. "You should be," Dong said.

She leaned towards him. "I happen to like foxes."

Dong approached Riley, a strange growl coming from his throat. "You should be afraid." He grabbed Riley and jumped up to the treetops, running across them.

Riley squealed. "I must be in a dream," she said, smiling as the wind fluttered in her hair.

Was she having fun? "Are you sure you are dreaming?" Dong dropped her, letting her fall.

Riley reached up towards him. She looked scared, but her words belied that. "I trust you," she said.

Dong hesitated, then swooped down, catching her and spinning them both safely to the ground. His eyes stayed on hers. Despite her fear as she was falling to her death, she still chose to trust him? Where did this trust come from?

Riley touched his face. "You're my dream. Claim me." She planted a kiss on his cheek. An impulsive move.

Not knowing what else to do, Dong opened a portal and returned home. He dropped Riley off by her car. He waved his arms and Riley's few possessions appeared in the car. Dong then put his hands on Riley's arms and steered her towards the vehicle.

"I've had Jing'er arrange a place for you to stay. Your services are no longer required. Goodbye, Riley."

Riley wanted him; he wanted Riley. He could never have her. His cheek burned where her lips had touched him. Without another word, Dong shifted to fox form and fled into the woods.

And the last of the autumn leaves fell from the trees, bringing with it the first touch of winter.

Chapter 16

The first snowfall reminded Riley of Dong. She grumbled, sitting by the window watching the heavy white fluffy flakes fall. Her roommate, Beatrice, noticed as she called Riley's attention back to what they were doing. Decorating Christmas cookies. Riley scooted back to the low coffee table and looked at the cookies. There were star shapes, stockings, canes, and Christmas tree shapes.

"I think we may have made too many," Beatrice said, cookie in hand.

"We'll just have to find more people to give some away to," Riley said.

"Do you know that many people?" Beatrice pointed to the assortment of cookies.

"No," Riley said.

"We could give some to—"

"I don't think so," Riley said, spreading some green frosting on a tree-shaped sugar cookie.

"But you were just thinking about him," Beatrice said.

Riley raised an eyebrow at her only friend and now roommate. "I was thinking of who?"

Beatrice pouted. "That dumb fox."

"I wasn't," Riley lied. She had been thinking about Dong. He was often in her thoughts. Was he doing okay? Did he miss her? She had to stop thinking about him.

Beatrice put her star-shaped cookie down. She had painted it with pink frosting.

"He's not being reasonable," Beatrice said. "He ruffles my feathers!"

Riley laughed. Beatrice had a knack for making her smile, a talent most welcomed.

Beatrice shared a small pout before brightening to a smile. "That's why I like you! You don't let things keep you down."

"And I like you," Riley said. "And not just for bailing me out of trouble."

Beatrice waved a hand. "That was nothing."

"To me it was something—everything, even."

Beatrice reached out a hand and placed it on Riley's and gave a gentle squeeze. "I liked you the moment I met you. So I wanted to help. I will help you with anything you need, just ask."

"Thank you," Riley said.

The pair continued to frost and box cookies. She eventually decided that she'd keep a dozen for her and Beatrice and boxed up the others in baker's dozens to hand out to neighbors. She pretended to be happy as they knocked on doors and handed out their cookies.

"We're your new neighbors and just want to drop off some holiday cheer," she said over and over. They were thanked and welcomed into the neighborhood. At the last apartment, a young man answered the door. Riley handed him the box.

"Why don't you come in?" he asked. "I can make some hot chocolate."

Beatrice eyed him carefully and decided she didn't like him, not one bit. "No. We can't stay," Beatrice said. "We have some more cookies to deliver."

"But thank you," Riley said, turning to leave.

"Wait," the man called. When Riley paused he said, "My name is Lucas. Might I ask yours?"

"Nope," Beatrice said, wanting to turn both her and Riley into birds to fly quickly away.

Riley glanced up at him long enough to reply. "Riley," she said.

"Riley," Lucas repeated. "I'll call on you."

Riley gave a small nod, not paying attention, for she had already returned to her innermost thoughts of silence.

Beatrice, on the other hand, was making a series of bird-like noises under her breath. "This would never do," she muttered in bird. It wasn't Riley's fault that she was beautiful and attracted men's attention, for she did seem to turn heads. She just didn't turn the head and heart of that darn fox. Beatrice would have to give him a piece of her mind.

"I'm going to go for a walk," Riley said, pulling Beatrice's attention back to her. "I'll see you later at home."

"Okay." Beatrice nodded. She watched Riley a moment, before transforming and flying up into the sky.

It wasn't the first time that Beatrice asked herself what was she going to do with Riley. The empress had sent her to help Riley and that horrible fox. Beatrice had thought all was good. Dong had stopped his tricks to get rid of Riley and even seemed to be smiling and laughing more. And then, what had happened? The next thing Beatrice knew, Riley had been kicked out! With no explanation. Jing'er, the stupid fox's sister, had reached out to her, reporting that Riley hadn't gone to the apartment they arranged for her and asked for help.

Beatrice had gone to the empress and quickly found Riley. Money shouldn't have been a problem, but Riley wouldn't touch the money that Dong had arranged for her. Beatrice, however, had no issue taking the fox's money.

Well, it was time Beatrice went to talk to Dong. That fox really could be bird-brained! She returned home, grabbed a box of cookies, and soared over to Fox Hill.

Beatrice knocked on the window of Dong's study. He glanced up, and ignored her?! She couldn't believe it. She knocked on it again. Dong got up and closed the curtain. Oh, her feathers were really ruffled now. She would just have to be rude then, so she ignored common courtesy and just portaled through the window, assuming human form and sitting on Dong's desk. The box of cookies on her lap.

"Jing'er, we need to get a cat," Dong called loudly.

Beatrice snorted. "Really? Like foxes don't eat birds."

"You'd be particularly nasty to cat," Dong said.

"I think the same of you," Beatrice said. "I really don't understand what she sees in you."

Dong's eyebrow rose, but he remained focused on his reading.

Jing'er was soon at the doorway. "Oh, it's that songbird. I'm leaving this to you, brother. I don't think a cat will solve your problem."

"It won't," Beatrice said, chin held high.

Jing'er's eyes noticed the box. It had a sweet smell to it. "What's this?"

"Oh, someone made these for *him.*" Beatrice opened the box, revealing the goodies inside.

"Cookies?" Jing'er asked. "May I?"

"Go ahead," Beatrice said, standing up and handing the box to Jing'er. As Jing'er took it, Dong got up and took it from both of them.

"Riley made these?" he asked.

"She did," Beatrice said.

Dong walked back to his desk with the box. "I helped," Beatrice said.

Dong glanced at her briefly before resuming his careful inspection of the cookies. "I can tell which one's were hers." He took several out and tossed the rest and the box aside.

"I'll take these ones," Jing'er said. "Riley made us cookies?" With a smile, she hugged the box. "No one has ever made me cookies." Jing'er turned to Beatrice. "You must thank her for us."

"You can thank her yourself," Beatrice said.

"I'll do just that," Jing'er said, leaving the room.

With only Beatrice and Dong left in the room, the fairy glared at him. "You are a big fat meanie," Beatrice said, fists clenched at her side.

Dong blinked at her. What had he done to deserve that, he wondered?

Beatrice wasn't done. "You don't deserve Riley!"

"That we can both agree on," Dong said. Maybe the bird was finally becoming sensible.

"The empress thinks otherwise, for some reason."

"I don't care." Or did he? Dong wasn't sure about anything anymore.

"Riley thinks otherwise," Beatrice said. "And you abandoned her. And now another man is taking your place!"

"What?" Dong said.

"Riley met someone today. His name is Lucas."

Dong stiffened. "Well, good for her. Now if you will leave me, I've got work to do."

"Fine!! Bird-brained stupid fox! I'm leaving!" In a puff of blue sparkles, Beatrice returned to her bird form and flew off.

Dong found, to his dismay, that he couldn't concentrate on his work anymore. He picked up one of the cookies and took a deep breath. Riley's scent was the primary one on the cookie. He studied it. It was shaped like a Christmas tree. Was it getting to be that time of the year already? Maybe he shouldn't have sent her off so abruptly. But what else could he do? She hadn't been scared to learn he wasn't human. She had still wanted him.

Claim me.

Those had been her words.

They had started feeling like a family, that last month in particular. He'd been happy. The yearning for a family that he had felt for so long was finally being filled.

And that scared him. Rather badly in fact.

Family was everything he wanted; everything he longed for. But family, while the greatest treasure, could also be the deadliest weapon.

He would live forever, in some form. Fox spirits like him, were immortal creatures. Humans had had various beliefs, but their souls were immortal. They however left the realms for some sort of paradise after they died. For all Dong knew, only mortals could go to that heaven. It reasoned, that eventually, he'd have to part with Riley.

Better to do that now, before he loved her too deeply to let her go. Before the pain was too great.

Why did his decision hurt so badly?

"Hey, Riley! Wait up," Lucas called, jogging up to Riley. "I thought it was you."

Riley politely nodded in greeting, but she kept walking along the sidewalk.

"Are you heading anywhere in particular?" Lucas asked, flashing a smile.

Riley shook her head. "No, not really."

"I should apologize," Lucas said.

Riley stopped walking and turned to face him. "Why?"

Lucas toed some snow with his foot, before looking up at Riley. "It was presumptuous of me to invite you and your friend in for hot chocolate. It's just, no one has ever welcomed me to the neighborhood before, much less dropped off freshly baked cookies." Lucas blew his hands and rubbed them together, before stuffing them in his pockets. "How about this, I'll treat you to your choice of coffee or cocoa. There's a lovely shop up this way in town."

"Oh, I don't know," Riley said. She didn't want to go. She just wanted the cold to numb her for a while.

"My hands are freezing," Lucas said. "And, I won't take no for an answer. Where's your friend?"

"We're meeting up at home later," Riley said.

Lucas nodded, placing a hand behind Riley's shoulder, leading the way. "I expected you two to be together when I raced after you."

"I wanted to be alone," Riley said. She still did. But she was cold, she realized.

"Should I go then?" Lucas asked.

Riley shook her head. "No, I think hot chocolate would be nice. It's been a rough couple of days—weeks. I don't even know."

They crossed the street and Lucas held open the door of the coffee shop. "What has a pretty girl like you losing track of time? What's his name?"

"Dong," Riley said.

At the same time, Lucas said, "I'm sorry, I shouldn't have asked that."

"It's okay," Riley said, taking off her coat and placing it on the back of a chair. Lucas placed their orders.

"Did you want to talk about it?"

"I don't know," Riley said. "He was the first boy I loved."

"Ah, that's a tough one," Lucas said.

Riley nodded. "I thought things were going well. I confessed to him and he kicked me out."

"You were living together?" Lucas asked.

"You could say that," Riley said, as the waitress brought them their hot chocolates.

"That sucks," Lucas said.

"What about you?" Riley asked.

"Huh, what about me?" Lucas took a sip of his chocolate.

"You said you've never been welcomed to the neighborhood before. Have you moved around a lot? How long have you been living in town?"

"Ah." Lucas laughed. "Let's see. I've moved around a bit the last few years, trying to find some ... steady work. I saw an ad for a handyman out here, so I packed up my belongings and moved to town. Lucky for me, too. Which is how I found you."

They talked for a while, over hot chocolate, Riley not really seeing her surroundings. It was a cozy shop, with teapots and teacups on various shelves. The wallpaper was cheerful.

When they were done, Lucas walked Riley home. "I hope I can see you again," Lucas said, dropping her off at the door.

"We live in the same building," Riley said. "I'm sure we'll see each other here and there."

"That's not exactly what I meant," Lucas said.

"Well, thank you for the hot chocolate." Riley smiled and slipped into her apartment. She hung her coat up in the closet and was closing it when she noticed Jing'er sitting on the couch.

"Hello, Riley," Jing'er said. "Nice place you have here."

Beatrice came out of the kitchen carrying some tea. "I'm sorry," she mouthed.

Jing'er smiled. "I ran into Beatrice today, so I thought I'd stop by for a visit. I hope you don't mind."

Chapter 17

Jing'er sat on the second-hand, but still comfortable, avocado green couch, eying the door with suspicion. "Who was that?"

"Just a neighbor," Riley said. "Have you been well?" This was most definitely awkward. How did she talk to Jing'er? And why was she there?

Jing'er nodded, skepticism evident on her face. "Right, just a neighbor." She glanced at Beatrice.

Beatrice poured a cup of tea for Jing'er and set the teapot on the coffee table. "We only met him today."

The fox accepted the cup. She took the spoon up and stirred it. "Peppermint?"

"If it pleases you," Beatrice said, rolling her eyes. She took a seat with a flop. The old blue recliner protested with a creaky thump.

"Bea! What's up with you?" Riley whispered.

"Nothing," the fairy said. "But Miss Fox asked for tea and all we had was peppermint, so that's what I offered. She already knew the answer. Besides, I'm being hospitable."

Jing'er laughed, amused. Her mirth didn't last long. "I don't like him."

Riley bristled and took a seat. "Nobody asked you." As far as Riley was concerned, Jing'er really had no say in who she was friends with.

Beatrice's eyes went wide, glancing between the fox and the girl.

"How did you find me?" Riley asked. If she were to admit it to herself, it gave her hope that Dong would show up and ask her to move back home.

Jing'er straightened up and smiled, casting a slight glance in Beatrice's direction. "A little bird told me."

Beatrice gasped and stood up. "I did not! She must have followed me."

Jing'er was laughing again. "Don't get your feathers all rumpled. Riley, I've known all along where you went."

"Does he know?" Riley asked.

"You go straight to that?" Jing'er shrugged. "He hasn't even asked where the apartment we arranged for you is. Why didn't you just stay there? He'd easily know where you were then."

Riley's heart ached. "I'm not looking for handouts." So, Dong didn't know where she was. What was worse was he didn't even care to know. She blinked back sudden tears.

Jing'er looked inordinately pleased and took another sip of tea. "This is really refreshing."

"You can show yourself out when you've finished," Beatrice said, indicating the door.

"I'm going to ignore that," Jing'er said. "Riley, you can't date that ... man." The way she said *man* was dripping with distaste.

Riley stood. She didn't want to socialize with Jing'er, nor did she want to pretend to be okay. "I'm going to apologize. I'm getting a headache, so I am going to go to lay down."

Jing'er stood up and placed her hand on Riley's arm. "I'm serious. If you really care about my brother the way I think you do, don't give up on him."

Riley didn't know how to respond. After a moment she changed tactics. "I have to get ready to leave, actually."

Beatrice was surprised. "Why? I thought we were watching movies tonight. You know, to keep your mind off of..." her voice dropped to a stage whisper, "a certain someone."

"I have a date tonight," Riley lied, talking a bit too loudly to cover up Beatrice's voice.

"What?!?" Jing'er and Beatrice were both shocked.

"With who?" Beatrice asked, suddenly suspicious.

"It's a blind date," Riley said.

"At least it's not that neighbor," Jing'er said.

"So what if it is?" Riley yelled. "Don't I deserve a chance at happiness and to be loved in return? No, because apparently, something is wrong with me! The one I want can't stand having me around. But Lucas is interested in me. Is that so wrong?"

Beatrice shook her head. "It's not."

"But he's not—" Jing'er protested.

Riley cut them off. "If you'll both excuse me, I'm going to go get ready."

Riley stomped off to her room and shortly after came out wearing a knee-length red dress with high heels. She had put her long hair in a bun, with a few loose curls framing her face. Jing'er had to admit, she looked lovely, even though she was showing quite a bit of leg. Modern girls had some pretty dresses, but they did seem a bit skimpy at times.

"Are you going out like that?" Jing'er asked.

Riley nodded.

"Is that the dress you got for the Christmas party?" Beatrice asked.

Riley pivoted to show off her dress. "Yes. How does it look?"

"It looks great," Beatrice said.

"It's a shame you are wearing it now though," Jing'er said.

"Why is that?" Riley asked.

"You shouldn't wear a dress to an event more than once."

Riley nearly laughed. "What silly rule is that?"

Jing'er gave a long-suffering sigh. "It's not a silly rule. But, if you want to make an impression and find a marriage match, you don't wear the same gown to more than one ball. You want to shine."

"You do realize what year it is?" Beatrice said. "People don't do that anymore."

"Whose side are you on?" Jing'er asked. "I'm trying to help."

"I've called Lucas to pick me up," Riley said. "He should be here in a few minutes. You two be good."

"Of course," Beatrice said.

Jing'er frowned. "I thought this was a blind date?"

"Uh, it is. I don't know where I'm going. I'll be wearing a blindfold. So it's a literal blind date." Riley cringed. She had never been a good liar, so she had never lied this much before. Fortunately, a knock at the door saved her. Beatrice and Jing'er gathered at the door, clamoring for a look.

"Why hello," Lucas said, his eyes landing on Jing'er. She smiled and winked at him. "Who might this be?"

Riley glanced at where Jing'er stood with Beatrice behind her. "This is my roommate's friend. She came into town to surprise Beatrice. I felt like a third wheel, so..."

Lucas lifted his chin in acknowledgment. "So that's why you called me."

Jing'er glanced at Riley. So, Riley had called Lucas.

Riley laughed lightly and gave Lucas a push towards the door. "Don't wait up for me," she called over her shoulder.

"Don't stay out too late," Beatrice said.

"I won't. Night!" Riley said, closing the door behind her. Once outside, she exhaled. "Thank you for bailing me out."

"Of course. I'm getting a date out of this right? So where are we going?" Lucas pointed towards his car. "I'm parked over there. Unless you wanted to drive?"

"No, that's okay. My car isn't that reliable."

"Gotcha. So, there's this little bar downtown. I heard a little local band is playing there tonight. Did you want to go?"

"A bar?" Riley said. "What about a movie?"

"But you're all dolled up. Let me show you off a bit," Lucas said. "It'll take your mind off your troubles to be a princess for the night."

"You think so?" Riley asked.

"I know so."

Riley smiled tentatively. "Okay."

Chapter 18

J ing'er was waiting in Dong's library when he got back from his run. He nodded once in greeting, picked up the book he was reading, and sat down in his chair by the window. The very window he had passed through to catch Riley when she fell off the ladder. His arms tingled just thinking about how she had felt in his arms. He wished he could hold her again. Hold her, and never let go. And to think, she wanted him.

Claim me.

Did she even know what she was asking? She wasn't a possession in need of an owner. He was dangerous. In his embrace, he could drain her life essence. At the worst, she'd be dead and he'd have damned his soul to the abyss. The only fitting place to be if he harmed Riley.

You're my dream.

Why hadn't his tactic to scare her away worked? In a small way, he was glad it didn't scare her. It hadn't scared Jinxia either, and she had lived in a time when nine-tailed foxes were acknowledged as real.

Why was he still thinking about this? Then he realized, he could smell Riley on Jing'er.

"You went and saw her again?" It was more a statement than a question.

"I did."

Dong grunted and opened his book. He didn't notice the book was upside down.

Jing'er did, however, and smiled. "Did you wish to know how she is doing?"

Dong cleared his throat. Jing'er said nothing, so Dong blinked and looked at the words on the page. They looked funny. After a moment he focused enough to realize the problem and turned his book right side up. His patience was fading fast and still Jing'er remained silent. "Are you going to tell me or not?"

"She's fine," Jing'er said. "Things seem to be going well for her."

"That's good," Dong said. Maybe he should stop by. It'd been a while since Jing'er had started visiting with her. Seven whole days, not that he was counting.

"She's living with that bird, you know."

"You've mentioned that." He turned a page.

"Don't you want to know where she is staying?" Jing'er asked.

"Didn't you make the arrangement as I asked?"

"I did, but—"

Dong cut her off. "As long as she is safe and happy, that's all that matters. Her severance pay will support her for some time to come since she won't have to worry about money." He'd find a way to provide support for her whole life, somehow. Maybe Jing'er could buy her a fake lottery ticket and he'd fund the winnings. That idea seemed good to him. He'd never be able to spend all the money he had before he left this realm. He didn't plan to stay there forever. Just for however long he needed to watch over Riley.

"How are things going between her and that... what's his name? That idiot?"

Jing'er smirked. "Brother, I do believe you are jealous."

Dong waved his hand in protest. "Not really. He is an idiot, wouldn't you agree?"

Pressing her lips together thoughtfully, Jing'er paused before answering. "At first I did."

"What changed your mind?"

"You, brother. I think you are more of an idiot."

Dong frowned, setting his book aside. "I'm going for another run. Don't wait up."

"Don't worry, I won't." Jing'er waved him off.

Dong ran into his woods before deciding he would look for Riley. Maybe actually seeing her would help put her out of his mind. How often he thought of her was alarming. And the thoughts were always wondering how she was doing. To make matters worse, everything in his home caused her to come to his mind. His room. His library. His kitchen. Yes, he would have to do it. Seeing that Riley was safe and happy would alleviate all the worry he had and he could get on with his solitary life. Turning around, he headed back towards the town.

It took him a while to locate Riley. He really should have asked Jing'er where the housing she arranged was. He had felt it was better he didn't know, but now it bothered him that he had entrusted that detail to Jing'er. He hadn't been thinking straight, that was certain. But, he also knew that deep down he could trust Jing'er with Riley. Right? Oh my goodness, he was going insane!

Riley was outside a Christmas tree farm. She was smiling and laughing as another man was securing a tree to the top of her car. Dong frowned. That must be him. An intense desire to drain the man of his energy overwhelmed him and he stepped closer. He'd have to make Riley sleep so he didn't scare her. He was almost close enough where he could catch her when she lost consciousness, he reached out to touch her shoulder and—

"Dong Lee!" Beatrice yelled.

Riley jumped, startled. She recovered quickly.

Lucas looked over at Dong. "So you're him."

Dong drew up short as Riley greeted him. Then she was introducing him. "This is my former boss, Mr. Lee," Riley was saying. He opened his mouth to speak and Riley held up a hand and gestured towards the man with her.

"Dong Lee, this is Lucas ..." Her voice trailed off. Dong was relieved that she didn't have a last name for this clod.

Lucas held out his hand. "It's Wróżka, Lucas Wróżka. Pleased to meet you, Dong."

"Mr. Lee," Dong said, correcting him.

Lucas acquiesced. "Mr. Lee."

Riley was studying his face. Was her rose-colored cheeks because of the cold or because of him? He frowned when he wondered if it was for Lucas. Drat, those darn rules.

He'd almost broken them. He'd have to thank Beatrice later. That bird was good for some things, as it turned out. The little blue fairy, he realized, was hanging around Riley. He had a spy. He could keep tabs on his Riley without risking falling deeper in love—no, without risking accidentally killing her on their wedding night. Wait, did he just—?

"Have you been well," Riley was asking.

Dong nodded. It was his turn to ask. "Have you been well? Eating well? Sleeping well?" He wanted to touch her cheek. To check her temperature, that is.

"Mostly," Riley said.

"I ... ah, meant to thank you for the cookies," Dong said.

Beatrice nudged him as Riley cast a sideways glance at the bird. Dong grinned. Yes, the bird would be most helpful.

"You're welcome." Riley took something out of her coat pocket. It was her keys. "I really should be going. I'm already late dropping off this tree."

"Did you need help?" Dong asked.

Riley looked at the ground. "Lucas is helping me out."

Dong frowned at Lucas. That wouldn't do at all. He turned to Beatrice and impressed upon her mind that her life depended on what she did next.

Beatrice suddenly clutched her stomach. "Oh-oh, it hurts!"

Riley bent over her friend, rubbing her back. "What's wrong?"

"My stomach," Beatrice said. "I need to get home."

Riley looked back at Dong and Lucas.

"Oh ohhh," Beatrice said. "I just need some brown sugar water. I'll be fine when I get home. Lucas, can you be a dear and take me home?"

"What about the tree? Riley?" Lucas asked. Beatrice moved closer to Lucas and collapsed so close he was forced to catch her.

"I'll help Riley," Dong said. "Besides, I need to talk to her."

Beatrice waved for Riley to go. "I'll be fine. Go on and don't worry about me."

Riley was suddenly all business. "If you are coming, Dong, get in." She opened the door to her car and climbed in.

Dong gave a triumphant grin to Lucas and walked to the passenger side, getting into the vehicle. Using the side view mirror, Dong watched as Lucas had Beatrice climb onto his back.

Riley put the car into gear and they were off.

Chapter 19

They drove in silence for a while. This gave Dong the perfect opportunity to study Riley's profile. His eyes kept traveling to her lips as he remembered her kiss. What would kissing her lips be like? He wanted to know. He stiffened. This was a bad idea.

"My driving isn't that bad," Riley said.

Clearing his throat, Dong turned his attention to the back of the road. It was bad timing because the car in front

slowed suddenly and Riley had to slam on her brakes. Between the slushy road and the tree's weight on top, Dong realized that Riley wouldn't be able to stop in time. Dong was about to utter some choice swear words, but Riley beat him to it with a growl. Did she just say *grr*? No time to wonder, he had a split second to react. He'd use up some of his spiritual energy doing this, but—he held up his hand and shoved the car in front of them off to the side. Riley managed to slide safely to a stop, and the car behind them rear-ended them. The tree atop the car came loose, dropping down to block the windshield.

"This is just great," Riley muttered, seeming to forget Dong was there. "I finally get to see him again and I get in a car accident. Is fate trying to tell me to give up?" Shaking her head Riley leaned over and reached for the glove box. Dong jumped back, well, as much as his seat let him. As Riley pulled some things out, a small package fell out of the compartment. Riley sighed.

"What are you doing?" Dong asked.

"I'm getting my insurance information. I have to swap it with the other driver." Riley got out of the car. "Plus, I want to make sure both of the other drivers are okay."

"Have you done this before?" he asked.

"No," Riley said. "This is my first accident."

Dong followed her out of the car. The first driver seemed stunned but was okay. The driver that rear-ended Riley apologized. There was no damage to any of the cars. Riley agreed to let her being rear-ended go. The other drivers were quickly off.

"I need a moment," Riley said. She was trembling.

Dong took the time to fix and secure the tree. When he was finished, Riley still hadn't moved. "I'll drive," he said, gently.

Riley handed him her keys and got in the passenger seat, putting away her insurance papers and picking up the small package, which she set on her lap, as she did so.

"I had forgotten about this," Riley said. She smoothed the box, her name written on it in a flowing elegant script.

Dong started up the car and pulled into the road. "Where to?"

"Uh, home I guess."

Dong glanced at her, concerned. "What about the tree?"

"Oh, I'm dropping that off at the library. It's for the giving tree."

"The giving tree?" Dong wasn't sure what that was.

"Yeah. Every winter the library has a giving tree to help needy families. They do it along with the local churches."

"How did you get involved?"

"Job seeking at the library," Riley said.

Dong felt a flash of shame, then anger. Had he really not given her enough money to get by? He was about to ask when Riley seemed to sense his reaction.

"I didn't touch the money you gave me as severance," Riley said. "I wanted to return it, but ... I haven't."

"Why?" Questions ran through his mind. Was it not enough? Should he give her more? Had it been too much?

Riley turned her attention back to her box. "It made being fired and not seeing you ever again seem too real."

Dong turned his gaze to her.

"And really, I could probably live a year on that and still have money left."

"It was the least I could do," Dong said.

"Yeah, well it wasn't what I wanted." Riley turned away and looked out the window.

"What do you want?" He would give her anything she wanted that was in his power to give.

Riley ignored him.

He tried again. "Riley. Tell me what it is that you want. Anything."

"Anything?" she asked, her finger tapping a snowflake through the window.

Dong swallowed, suddenly unsure. Maybe this wasn't a good idea, but he'd never given a severance before when firing someone. That was something that just wasn't done. If you had failed in your duties, you got fired. That was that.

Riley spoke quietly. "I told you. And you threw me away."

"I'd never throw—" He stopped. He had thrown her out. Out of his house. Out of his life. But that red string of fate that kept him thinking about her, must still be causing her to think of him.

Riley turned to look at him. Were those tears? Dong's heart knotted up. Riley's voice did not waver when she spoke. "I think I'm in love with you. No, I know I am. Exactly what do I mean to you?"

You're everything to me, he thought. But he couldn't bring himself to say it. Instead, he said, "Let's drop this tree off, and then I'll take you home."

Lucas helped Beatrice settle into the couch. He fetched her blanket. "You'll be okay? Do you need me to get you anything?"

"I'm fine," Beatrice said. "Seriously. It's only a little tummy ache."

"I was a little worried," Lucas said. "My sister would get terrible cramps. I'll brew the brown sugar water for you. Where do you keep the sugar and ginger?" He walked into the kitchen and started opening doors.

"Um," Beatrice said. She wasn't sure they had any. "We might be out. It's okay though, I'm fine."

"I think I have some at my place," Lucas said. "I'll be right back."

"Uh, okay." Beatrice wasn't sure what to think. Her stomach pain was probably guilt from lying and abandoning Riley with that fox. But, while she knew that Dong could be dangerous, she knew that he'd not deliberately hurt Riley. Why he was fighting being with Riley was beyond the fairy's comprehension. And what about Lucas? He wasn't exactly human, Beatrice was sure of that. But exactly what he was, she wasn't sure. It was blocked from her senses.

It was while Beatrice was lost in thought that Riley came home. The first thing Riley did was check on her friend. "How are you feeling?"

"Oh, I'm okay. How did things go with that fox?" Beatrice replied.

Riley sat down on the couch next to Beatrice. "It went okay I guess. No, it didn't go good at all."

"What happened?"

Riley told Beatrice everything.

"That stupid fox. Sometimes I really want to peck his eyes out!" She jabbed the air with her hand a few times in emphasis.

Riley laughed. "I doubt that."

"Well, he makes me mad," Beatrice admitted.

A knock sounded at the door and Lucas let himself in. "I've made the brown sugar water," he said, bringing in a thermos. "How's our patient?" He winked at the girls. Beatrice frowned.

"I'll fetch a cup and you can ask her yourself," Riley said, getting up and heading to the kitchen.

"I said I was much better. It was only because of the fox," Beatrice muttered.

"Fox?" Lucas asked. "Don't tell me you ate a fox. They give me terrible stomach pain too. Very hard on the digestion."

Beatrice was about to say something when she realized that Lucas was teasing.

"I'm joking," he said. "I've never even hunted a fox. Foxes are one of the blessed animals, so it's forbidden to eat them."

"You say some strange things," Riley said, setting a cup down.

"It's an old family thing. I'll explain it to you one day." Lucas smiled as he poured the warm sugar tea for Beatrice. "There you go. No need to suffer."

"Thank you," Beatrice said, taking the offered cup.

"Oh, where did my box go?" Riley started to look around.

"What box?" Beatrice asked.

"I must have left it in my car. It was in my glove compartment. I had forgotten all about it. I'll be right back." Riley left to go retrieve it. But it was not in the car. And she couldn't find it at home. Had she lost it? Where had it gone?

Chapter 20

Dong was in his woods. He had run there upon returning home. It was now late into the night. The cold wintry air felt nice. It was almost numbing him. Almost. He felt guilty about Riley's box. He shouldn't have taken it, but ... he had felt magic emanating from it. He wanted to see what was in it before she did. He didn't trust that Lucas, not that Lucas gave him any reason to other than being near Riley. Would he trust anyone near Riley?

Maybe. No. Definitely no. He was going to hate whoever Riley chose for her husband. The thought came to him that he could arrange for her to be a widow. Foxes had been known to do that when lovers married someone else.

Snow crunched softly nearby. He sniffed the air. It was Jing'er. "What is it?"

"I've returned Riley's box to her."

"Where did you leave it?"

"On the dresser in her bedroom."

Dong turned to his sister. "How is she?"

Jing'er sat down by her brother, her tail swishing. "You've been out for a long time. I was starting to worry."

Dong growled. "Riley?"

Jing'er exhaled and shook her head. Her brother was definitely being an idiot. The woman actually wanted to be with him, and Dong was pushing her away. If that wasn't idiotic, Jing'er wasn't sure what was.

"Love doesn't make sense," Jing'er said. "It's a blessing to find it. You should just accept it and enjoy what time you are given."

Dong growled again.

Jing'er put up her paws in a rather human manner. "Riley is fine. She was sleeping and stayed sleeping. Even the bird didn't realize I was there."

Dong looked back out to the trees. "Keep an eye on her for me while I'm gone."

"Where are you going?" Jinger asked.

"To Celestial Ridge to seek answers."

"What do you mean?" What answers did Dong seek? Dong didn't keep her wondering long.

"Riley has been tied to me by the red string of fate. I want to know that she won't be hurt because of it when I leave. I want to give her, her life back." Dong glanced up at the falling snow. The flakes were large. Was it snowing by Riley? He shut his eyes, letting the flakes fall on his face.

The two sat there awhile, each in their own thoughts.

"You love her, brother." It wasn't a question.

"I ... I do care deeply about her. She is safer away from me though. What if I lose control?"

Jing'er studied him. "What do you mean?"

"There's a reason why there are stories of our kind killing brides and grooms."

So that was it. Dong was afraid he'd kill Riley. "Yes, but that is because some of our kind actually did."

"When I'm with Riley, it's difficult not to draw her energy in. I don't need her liver to take everything from her."

Jing'er laughed and Dong glared at her. "It's not an involuntary action to draw a human's energy in. You can control it. You also don't actually need a liver."

"Then why did we do it?" Dong asked.

Jing'er swished her tail. "It made it easier, in the beginning. It was also a fear tactic from ancient stories we used. Think about it. When you take in energy from the small game you hunt, do you need their liver or hearts? No, you even *let them live*."

Dong thought a moment. "You have a point."

Jing'er gave a toothy smile. "The liver was a calling card. Also, you only hunted criminals or those who were evil and deserved to die."

"Did I have the right to judge?"

"In the past, yes. When we were nobles. But not now," Jing'er said. Things were different now. Even she knew better.

"I am not sure we did even then."

Jing'er stood up. "Well, enough of this boring discourse. I have delivered the box back to your woman; she will be none the wiser for it's missing."

"Thank you, sister." Dong got up and placed his head low to the ground in the best bow a fox could do. Then he ran off.

For her part, Jing'er watched him go, feeling a certain empathy for him. It wasn't easy to truly love someone. You put that person first, and he was certainly putting Riley's happiness above his own. But she was worried. When they did marry, was it possible he could accidentally kill her? Maybe those foxes hadn't *all* done it on purpose. Some might have, but all of them? There had to be a way to protect a mortal lover. Dong would figure it out. She wanted Dong to be with the one he loved. Now, how could she help Dong and Riley get together? This time, she had to get it right.

Riley was pulling a shirt out of her dresser when she noticed the small box sitting on top. "How did this get here?" Why didn't she remember putting it there? Her name was in her mother's handwriting. Taking the treasure with her, she went and sat on her bed. When her aunt had thrown her out, she had forgotten about it. It had arrived as her last gift from her parents. Opening the box, Riley took out the contents. A small, nearly white, jade ring, a set of matching earrings, and a matching flat jade oval, about the size of a monocle. It had a small chain of smaller jade stones.

"Beatrice," Riley called. "Come look at this."

Beatrice took a seat on the bed. "What is it?"

"It's what my parents left for me."

Beatrice lightly touched the earrings. "These are lovely." She looked at the ring.

"This almost looks like a monocle," Riley said, holding the flat piece of jade up to her eye. She meant it as a joke, for she had no idea what the stone was. But when she looked at her friend thought it, she gasped. "You're a bird!"

"What?" Beatrice was startled. She looked over her arms and spun around trying to see behind herself.

Riley put the stone down, then looked back through it again. "This is amazing!"

"Riley, be serious."

"I am. No wonder you say such odd things. And can whistle like a songbird. Oh my gosh. How many magical creatures are real? Besides nine-tailed foxes that is. Can you all become human?"

Beatrice held out her hand. "Can I see that stone?"

"Sure," Riley said. When she dropped it into Beatrice's hand, Beatrice tested it out.

"I don't see anything when I look through it. It's solid as a rock. But, it does seem to have some inner power. It's faint and fading." She held it out to give back. When Riley's fingers touched it, a flash of power went through it with a crackle. Beatrice gave out a small cry and dropped the stone.

"Are you okay?" Riley asked, picking up the piece of jade.

Beatrice nodded. "I am. I felt a jolt of electricity when you touched it. It was like it flared to life."

Riley looked at the stone. "I didn't feel anything. I wonder what the other items do." Riley picked up the earrings and put them on. "I don't see anything special. Maybe they aren't magical like the stone." She put the ring on. It was a perfect fit. "Well, even if these are normal items, the monocle is totally amazing. When were you going to tell me you were a bird?"

"I'm not a bird," Beatrice said. "I'm a bird fairy. And I wanted to tell you."

"I have so many questions. So, you know what Dong and Jing'er are?"

"Of course," Beatrice said. "The real question is do you?"

Riley grinned. "Sometimes when you referred to him as a fox it would make me smile despite my sadness. I know. He's a nine-tailed fox. I didn't just fall in love with a regular guy, mine is an adorable fox. My nine-tailed fox."

"Riley, how much do you know about nine-tailed foxes?"

"About as much as I know about bird fairies—next to nothing. So what's your true form? Is it what I see now or what I see when I look with my stone?"

"Both. I am as you see now, and a bird." Beatrice made a sweeping motion with her right arm, and amidst blue sparkles, she transformed into a small blue songbird. "I hatched as a bird, and as I grew I had two forms. I learned to control my life force to be the form I want." With another wave, she turned into a bird-sized human, then back to a bird, and finally to the woman that Riley knew and loved.

"I wish I was a fairy," Riley said. "Do you think it's possible I am?"

"It wouldn't be unheard of," Beatrice said. "Have you ever been to fairyland?"

"I think Dong took me," Riley answered. "But I'm not sure."

"I mean, by yourself."

"I don't think so. My parents died when I was young. I barely remember them." She only remembered the storm. The terrible and loud thunder. The glowing flashes of light. And a faint recollection— a red fox that had stayed with her. To that very day, thunderstorms rendered her hysterical.

Beatrice shrugged. "Maybe. I am sure we will find out. Wouldn't it be amazing if you were a bird fairy too?"

Riley nodded. But she was thinking she'd much rather be a fox fairy. A slow smile lit up her face and she blushed

Beatrice noticed. "You are thinking about him, aren't you?"

Riley grinned. "Is it that obvious?"

Beatrice gave Riley a playful pinch. "Yes."

"Tell me about him. About foxes."

Beatrice tilted her head. "Fox spirits are immortal."

"Dong told me, but I really didn't heed that. Do you think that is why he rejected me?"

Beatrice shrugged. How was she supposed to know what that devil was thinking? "You'll have to ask him."

Chapter 21

R iley stood on the porch and bravely knocked on the
door of Fox Hill. She still had her key but didn't feel
right about using it. After a few minutes, when she was
about to give up, she heard movement inside.

Jing'er opened the door and smiled. "Riley! Do come
inside from the cold. Are you moving back in?" She looked
around and frowned when she didn't see a suitcase or
trunk. "Are the boxes in your car?"

"I'm not moving back in," Riley said, stepping into the foyer. "Is he home?"

Jing'er blinked. "He?" Jing'er knew exactly who Riley meant, but she meant to have a little fun. Besides, Dong was not at home. On top of that, he'd gone insane. It was interesting to Jing'er that he'd lost his marbles over Riley, who actually had wanted to be with him and was running away. Maybe she should help them make some ties that couldn't be undone. The first step would be getting Riley to stay.

Riley's cheeks turned brighter. "Dong. Is he home?"

"Not at the moment."

"Oh, I'll come back." Riley turned to back out the door, and Jing'er stopped her.

"Here, let me take your coat." Riley's coat and gloves were off before she could blink. Jing'er turned and put them in the closet. She smiled at Riley. "Follow me. We can chat while we wait for that brother of mine to return. I was just going to make some—" What exactly should she make, Jing'er wondered. Chocolate did wonders for human girls. "Chocolate brownies. Care to help?"

"Sure, I can help." It's not like Riley had anywhere to be, as she did want to talk to Dong.

"I like your earrings," Jing'er said, her eyes noticing the small jade earrings.

Riley touched her ears. "Thank you. I just got them. They were my mother's."

"They look like white jade." Jing'er reached out to touch one but stopped. No, she realized, that would be rude. She withdrew her hand. Riley didn't seem to notice.

115

Jing'er set to work fetching a large mixing bowl. "I don't remember my mother. I never knew her. What was yours like?"

Riley gathered the eggs, cocoa powder, powdered milk, brown sugar, and oil. "I was very young when she died. What I do remember is that she was beautiful, fun, and kind. She would take me on walks in the woods. I still love going to the woods." Riley closed her eyes, smiling. A lone tear gathered at the corner of her eye. "We'd play hopscotch together."

"Hopscotch?"

Riley nodded. "It's a game of jumping. You draw a board and alternate between jumping on one foot or two." She demonstrated on her way to the pantry, where she grabbed the small bottle of vanilla extract and molasses.

"Ah, I know that one." Jing'er was pleased with how at home Riley still was in the kitchen.

"Her favorite time of the year was Christmas. We'd walk and enjoy the pretty lights together."

"It is a very pretty holiday. But don't you like the mysterious and eerie Halloween?" Jing'er gave a small growl and held her hands like paws scratching the air.

"Halloween can be fun," Riley agreed. "But Christmas is my favorite. Especially if it snows."

"Ah, so you like that white stuff? Some years we'd see so much snow and food would get scarce. It's not my favorite at all."

"Does Dong like Christmas?" Riley started measuring and putting ingredients in the bowl.

Jing'er leaned on the counter and thoughtfully chewed on her lower lip. "You'd have to ask him. I don't think he has a reason to not like it. He didn't have to spend the last many years living as an ordinary f—" Jing'er stopped abruptly, her cheeks coloring.

"Did you have to spend years living as an ordinary fox?" Riley asked.

Jing'er nodded, then stopped. "Wait, what did you say?"

"Dong told me what you are. Didn't he tell you?"

Jing'er was surprised. "You remember that?"

"Of course, why wouldn't I?"

Jing'er grinned and Riley, if she had noticed, would have stepped backwards. "Foxes such as us can influence the mind."

"So he could have hocus pocused me to forget?" Riley asked. "I'm glad he didn't. I would beat him up if he did that!" Riley waved a wooden mixing spoon as if it was a sword.

Jing'er laughed, a low hearty laugh. "You would so not win."

Riley placed her hands on her hips, the spoon still in her hand. "And why ever not? I have some surprising moves up my sleeves. I've seen some martial art films!" Riley pretended to fight an imaginary combatant. Jing'er couldn't hide her amusement. To her, it looked like a child playing.

"Dong is an extremely skilled fighter. You'd need to do better to beat him."

Riley stopped sparing. "Well, I might be able to arrange something to disarm him." Riley smiled dreamily, imagining hugging him, or maybe even a quick kiss.

"I can think of a few ideas, but you'd need to be married to him or you'd be in trouble."

"What do you mean?" Riley returned to the bowl and finished mixing the brownies.

"Well," Jing'er leaned over and whispered into Riley's ears. Riley's cheeks burned red.

Riley coughed and cleared her throat. "Well, fencing in the au naturel would definitely not work."

"Oh, it would." Jing'er grinned. If Riley took her suggestion, setting them up to spend the night together would be a lot easier. Ties that can't be undone and all that.

Riley chose to focus on the brownies and poured the batter into a well-greased pan.

Jing'er took the pan and put it in the oven. There, she had helped, Jing'er thought proudly. "Well, on that topic, I'd very much like you to be my sister. Call me *Xiǎo gū.*"

"*Xiǎo gū?*"

"That's it," Jing'er said. "*Xiǎo gū*, or *Xiǎo gū* Jing'er."

"Is that Chinese?"

"It is. If it's too hard, you can use *Jiějiě* or—Oh, I hear something. Is that you, brother?"

"Who else would I be?" Dong called back, closing the front door.

"Ok, so try it now." Jing'er pronounced it slow and quietly for Riley.

"*Xiǎo gū*," Riley said, just as Dong walked into the kitchen. He came to a dead stop.

Jing'er almost purred. "I'll be right back."

"Jing'er," Dong said in a low voice.

"We're making brownies," Jing'er called back. "Do be kind to my sister-in-law, will you?"

Riley was focusing on the floor, cheeks red. Well, this was awkward, wasn't it?

"Riley," Dong said, greeting her. He gave a slight bow of the head. "I won't be in your way long. Tell my little sister my request was granted and we can discuss our arrangements later." He then took a bottle of water from the fridge and left.

Jing'er popped her head back into the kitchen. "Follow him," she whispered, shooing Riley with her hands. "Go on."

Riley exhaled. Here goes nothing she thought. She had come to see Dong, and here he was. But, she was suddenly nervous. Well, there was no reward without risk.

Dong's heart rate wasn't going to settle down at this rate. Quiet, gentle footsteps approached, followed by a tentative knocking on the door.

"Dong, it's Riley. Can we talk?"

Of course, he knew it was Riley. Not only could he hear her approach, but he could also smell her. And that sister of his, teaching Riley to address her as *sister-in-law*. *Xiǎo gū*. He'd have to talk to Jing'er about that. As much as he wanted it, he would never take Riley as his wife. The best way to protect her was to give her up. She'd find a new lover and forget him, right? He crushed his water bottle, water spraying like a volcano.

Another tentative knock.

"May I come in?" Riley tried again.

A quick burst of magic and he dried the spilled water. He looked up and answered. "Come in, Riley."

Riley walked in and Dong tried to not look up at her. He held his newspaper like a shield.

"You read the paper?" She laughed. "You could just use the internet."

"I prefer the feel of paper," he said.

"Mmm." She walked over to his bookshelf and started touching the spines of books as she looked over the titles. "I really admire your personal library."

"This is just a small portion of it," he said, absently. He was acutely aware of her. He stole a glance, her back to him.

Riley pulled out a book. "Chinese Myth and Legends," she read. "Does it talk about nine-tailed foxes?"

"Not really," Dong said. "We didn't just roam China in this world, inspiring stories, and legends."

"Mmm," Riley said again.

Mmm. If she'd turn to face him, he could see her lips while she made that sound. Why did he just think that? He needed to control his thoughts better.

Riley turned around at that moment. The book was open in her hands. The way the sun danced on her red-brown hair made her look angelic. Without thinking, Dong dropped his paper and found himself standing in front of Riley.

"Riley," he said.

She looked up at him, her beautiful eyes gazing into his. His eyes went to her lips. Maybe he could partake and not devour her.

No, he mustn't risk it.

He lost the battle raging in his heart, and his lips crashed down on hers. She felt so right in his arms. Arms that had a mind of their own. She dropped the book. It landed by his feet, so he kicked it away. One of his hands went into her hair, the other around her waist, pulling her closer. He discovered her shirt wasn't one that tucked in. Her skin was electric. He felt her qi surround him and mix with his.

He started to drink it in—and broke the kiss, retreating to the far end of the room. "I'm sorry," he said.

She approached. "I'm not. You know how I feel about you." She closed her eyes, her hand going to her forehead as she stumbled. A pallor lit her skin.

Dong cursed himself and quickly moved a seat for her to sit in. "Do you feel weak?" He tenderly helped her sit down.

She nodded. "They write in romance novels about getting weak in the knees with a kiss. I never expected it was true." She smiled, a little color returning to her face.

Dong shook his head. She didn't understand. How did he explain it to her? "In the past, many nine-tailed foxes would drink the inner energy, the life force, out of their lover. I started to do that—"

Riley furrowed her brow and shook her head. "No, I trust you. I've told you that."

"You shouldn't." He held his forehead, weary about having this same conversation with her again. She should not trust him. He could kill her.

"I choose to trust you."

"You don't know what you are choosing," Dong said.

Riley smiled. "Does anybody really know what they are choosing when they love? I feel safe with you. I love you. I want *you* to love *me*."

He wanted to grow old with her. For the first time, he hated that he was immortal, that any time he kissed her, he could go too far.

Dong's heart was in pain. He knew what he needed to do to keep Riley safe. What he must do.

"I'm leaving this world," he said, barely a whisper.

Her voice faltered. "What? Why?"

"I can't risk it." His voice was barely a whisper. This was excruciating.

"Risk what?"

"Causing you harm." Riley was within his arm's reach. Oh, how badly he wanted her to be his wife. His one and only true wife.

"What if your leaving causes me harm?" Riley asked.

Dong kept his eyes down. "How is that possible?"

Riley leaned towards him. "It will break my heart. I want to be with you forever."

He looked up. "Riley." It was all he managed. He blinked back a tear.

Riley pressed on. "Don't I have a say in who I want to be with?"

This is where he should tell her that she does have a choice, as long as it wasn't him. But he couldn't bring himself to say it. Instead, he ran away.

Riley stayed there for a while, before setting her key on his desk and leaving.

Jing'er watched Riley from the window, brownies baking in the oven.

Chapter 22

Jing'er ruminated all night on what to do regarding the situation. Her brother loved Riley but was being a halfwit over it. Just because the first time he loved someone hadn't worked out, didn't mean none would work out. Maybe it was time to tell Riley what had happened all those years ago. Would Riley still want to be her friend once she revealed her part? She hoped so. No one had wanted to be friends with her before. Sure, she could

charm people, but that wasn't a real friend. Riley had chosen her, without magical enchantments compelling her. Jing'er liked Riley, and she had been honest when she asked her to call her xiǎo gu.

Jing'er knocked on Riley's front door. Beatrice answered and let her in. "Riley's in the shower," Beatrice said.

"I brought the brownies." Jing'er handed Beatrice the box of baked goods.

Beatrice nodded, taking and setting them on the side table by the couch. "Riley could use the chocolate pick-me-up. What did that brother of yours say to her?" Beatrice sat down on the couch.

Jing'er followed the example and took a seat. "I'm not sure what is going on in his head. But I do know what's in his heart."

"Does he even have one?" Beatrice asked.

"Of course he does," Jing'er said. His heart was why he was struggling so much.

After a moment, Beatrice sighed. "Riley is usually so optimistic. Despite all her hardships, she keeps going. And she's faced a lot."

Jing'er knew that was one of the things that attracted Dong to Riley. "She's like an unstoppable ray of sunshine. It's one of the things I like about her."

Beatrice smiled at Jing'er. "She is sunshine."

A door opened and footsteps came down the hall. "Bea, I think I'll skip breakfast today if that's okay," Riley said coming into the living room. "Oh," she said, seeing Jing'er.

Jing'er smiled at Riley and pointed to the brownies. "I brought the brownies we were making. You left before they were done. Plus, I was worried."

Riley shifted on her feet. "Oh. I had remembered I had somewhere to be, so—"

"You forgot your key," Jing'er said, pulling it out of her pocket.

"I felt I should return it, you know."

"Can we talk?" Jing'er asked.

Riley put her hands in her pockets and took a seat on the edge of a chair. "Okay."

Jing'er glanced at Beatrice and indicated with an ever-so-sight-nod that she could leave.

"I have something to do, so I'll go so you can talk in private." Beatrice stood and hurriedly waved her arms, blue sparkles twinkled and she was gone.

Jing'er placed her hand on Riley's arm. "Are you okay? I mean really okay?"

Riley blinked back tears and shook her head. The expression of concern was such on Jing'er that it tore through the barrier Riley was trying to hold up. "No, I'm not."

Jing'er picked up the plate of brownies from the box. "Chocolate?"

Riley gave a small laugh and took one. "I'm sorry I ran off like that. I realize it was rude, but—"

Jing'er gently squeezed Riley's arm. "I understand. That brother of mine can be extremely dimwitted for being as old as he is."

"I don't know what to do," Riley said. "I've told him how I feel. I know he feels something for me." She unconsciously touched her lips with her hand that held the brownie. She didn't take a bite.

"He does love you."

"Then why does he keep pushing me away?" She set the brownie down and wiped away a tear.

"Remember when we were talking and I told you that long ago he had a sweetheart named Jinxia?"

Riley nodded. "You said you felt that was why he might be avoiding you."

Jing'er nodded. "As I told you, I didn't like that Dong had revealed to her what we were. It was okay if he wanted to court her. He'd have his fun, and we'd move on before they discovered what we were. But he told her what he was and asked her to marry him. I got angry and argued with him, told him he was being a fool. But it I who was the fool. And I harmed my own brother, nearly getting him killed."

"Jinxia. Dong told me he killed her."

Jing'er shook her head. "It was my fault. Jinxia was a marquis's daughter. At the time, my brother held a commandery post. Jinxia's brother was a soldier under his command, and a trusted brother-at-arms. The marquis didn't want Jinxia to marry Dong, and even forbid it. But she refused to eat or drink unless she was allowed to marry him, and he relented. Besides, he wanted to put his son in my brother's post. He'd then not only be the marquis, but he'd gain control of the army.

"Because she was frail, the marquis forbid them to consummate their marriage. Dong agreed as he had his concerns that he'd devour her life force. He sought a way to prevent it though, settling on a blood oath. That oath linked them in ways they didn't expect.

"Jinxia eventually learned of her father's plot to kill Dong and have her brother take his position. So she asked me to help her. She asked me to obtain a poison that she might drink and lay on the brink of death. She would appear to all that she was indeed dead. Her father would then bury her and go into mourning. Dong could then give her the antidote and take her away from there.

"But we didn't know the power of the oath Dong had made. Dong knew the moment Jinxia drank the poison, for he felt it. He rushed to her side. Because of the blood oath, when she was dying, so was he. The marquis used that moment to attack my brother. He was severely wounded, weakened by the poison. There was only enough antidote for one. To pay for what her father had done, Jinxia chose to revoke the oath, using her dying breath to do it. She gave Dong the antidote."

"What happened then?" Riley asked.

"He lived and she died," Jing'er said. "When he was in the care of the Celestial Empress, he said he would never forgive me. Hundreds of years passed by. This brings us to his less than ecstatic greeting when I showed up on his doorstep."

"Dong," Riley whispered.

Jing'er took Riley's hands into her own. "Please, don't give up on my brother. He loves you. I know it."

Riley was silent, but somehow, Jing'er knew Riley's answer, for Jing'er saw the red string of fate on Riley's hand glow. Riley wouldn't give up on Dong. She was strong, and she loved him unconditionally. If anyone could love that brother of hers, it was Riley.

Chapter 23

Riley looked in the mirror, double-checking that her hair and makeup looked okay.

Beatrice stopped behind Riley and looked in the same mirror. "You look beautiful, Riley. The real question is, how do I look?"

Riley surveyed her friend. Beatrice's golden hair was down to her waist. She wore some beautiful decorative hairpins. Her dark eyes sparkled, eyeliner enhancing their glorious darkness against her porcelain skin.

"I'm envious," Riley said.

"What? No, you can't be. I wish I had those dark auburn highlights that your pretty brown hair has. Besides, doesn't a certain devil like you? He'd eat me to be rid of me if he could."

"Don't say that, Bea. He wouldn't eat you."

Beatrice gave Riley a dubious look. "Foxes eat birds."

"Well," Riley said. She knew she couldn't really argue that point. But Dong wasn't really a fox, he was a spirit fox. That had to be different, right?

Beatrice started giggling. "By your expression, you just pictured him with a bird in his mouth. Was he man or fox?"

"It's not funny," Riley said, turning a tad green. "It's gross."

"And I'm the bird," Beatrice quipped. "Maybe you can give up on him now?"

Riley shook her head in protest. "I love him. I don't see that changing. Ever."

Beatrice put her hand on Riley's arm. "It's okay. Just don't decide to like that Lucas." Beatrice shuddered.

"What's wrong with Lucas?" Riley asked, taking a moment to grab her shoes.

"I get this feeling that something is off about him," Beatrice said.

Riley took a seat and put on the black pumps.

Beatrice followed. "Even Jing'er doesn't like him, but she isn't sure why. She says it's like her senses are dulled on him."

"Well, my heart is set on Dong. Despite everything. Do you think he'll be at the party?"

Beatrice shook her head. "It's a town Christmas party, so no. He avoids anything with the town."

With a sigh, Riley said, "I'll grab our gifts for the giving tree, and then we can go." She got her coat and picked up a box full of wrapped gifts.

"I'll grab the pies," Beatrice said. "I've never been to a Christmas party. I'm excited."

"I'm happy to be attending with you," Riley said.

When Riley stepped out of the apartment, hands reached out and took hold of the box of gifts.

"You have your hands full, let me get that for you," Lucas said.

"Oh, thank you." Riley let Lucas take the box out of her hands. This way she should see where she was walking and avoid getting snow in her shoes.

Lucas sized up the box. "I see you've been shopping."

"I think she enjoyed the giving tree a bit too much," Beatrice said.

Riley turned to Beatrice. "You think? Wasn't it you who also had to grab a couple of names?"

"How many kids did you two buy for?" Lucas asked.

"Riley picked three," Beatrice said.

Riley stood straighter. "I would have picked more if I could have. A child not having Christmas makes me sad."

"That was very generous of you," Lucas said. "Tell you what, my car has more room. I'll just set these in the trunk, and you ladies can ride with me."

"I don't think—" Beatrice said.

Lucas wasn't taking no for an answer. "I insist. The roads can get icy at night."

"Thank you," Riley said, glancing at Beatrice. She tried to let Beatrice know it was okay.

Beatrice gave a long-suffering sigh as Lucas opened the trunk and put the gifts inside. Walking around to the passenger side, he opened the car door. "Riley, your chariot awaits."

Riley smiled politely and climbed into the car. Shutting the door, Lucas turned to Beatrice and opened the back passenger door. "Miss Beatrice." Beatrice frowned and climbed in. As she did so, Lucas said, "Don't worry, Bea, on the way home you can ride shotgun."

"What?" Beatrice said as the door closed. What did he mean that? Beatrice would have to get Riley away from him so she could ask.

Holiday music was loudly playing in the large community room at the library. The giving tree was along the far wall, with a comfortable recliner waiting for a visit from Santa. A long table was set up along the adjacent wall, where the pot luck food was set out. At the next wall, was the dessert table. A happy buzz of chatter filled the room.

Lucas lead the girls to one of the tables. He pulled out a chair and indicated it was for Riley.

"Thank you," Riley said, accepting the seat.

Beatrice noticed and frowned at Riley.

Lucas chuckled and pulled out a second chair. Beatrice's frown deepened. Riley gave her friend an encouraging nod, so Beatrice took the seat.

"It seems I might be popular," Lucas said, taking a seat next to Riley.

Riley took a moment to look around. Sure enough, some of the single ladies were casting glances their way. One woman caught Riley looking and turned away, nose in the air. "I think so," Riley said. "Did you see that?"

"See what?" Lucas asked.

"The woman over there in the gaudy silver dress. She was looking at you with a flirty smile until she caught me eyeing her."

Lucas leaned in, his eyes sparkling. "I only have eyes for one woman," he whispered.

Flustered, Riley looked away. Beatrice made some displeased chirping noises.

"So, do you think that tyrant of yours is coming?" Lucas asked, sitting back in his chair.

"My what?"

"The guy you liked before you met me," Lucas said.

"I don't think so," Riley said. Still, she looked around the room, hopeful.

"Jing'er came," Beatrice said suddenly, patting Riley's shoulder. She hopped up and flapped her arms about. "Jing'er!!"

Jing'er smiled when she spotted them, making her way through the tables to Riley and Beatrice.

"May I sit with you?" Jing'er asked, eyes on Riley. Not waiting for a reply she took a chair and moved it between Riley and Lucas, forcing Lucas to move his chair.

"See, what did I tell you?" Lucas said to Riley.

"What did you tell?" Jing'er asked, taking her seat. She smiled up at Lucas and lowered her eyelashes enough to add a touch of coy shyness.

"That all the ladies want my attention," Lucas said. "But I've found the lady of my dreams." He cast a sideways glance at Riley.

"Oh?" Jing'er said. "Do I know this dream lady?"

Beatrice smiled and leaned closer to Riley to whisper. "Leave it to that fox. She'll get Lucas out of your hair."

"Why would I need him out of my hair?" Riley whispered back.

Beatrice shook her head. "Two of a feather, both bird-brained," Beatrice muttered. Suddenly smiling again she said, "Riley, come with me to get some food!"

"They haven't said grace yet," Riley said.

Clutching her stomach, Beatrice moaned. "I hope they hurry up. I'm starving."

Riley turned again, looking towards the door to see if Dong was coming. "I hope he comes," she said.

Jing'er gave a sad smile. "I came, Riley. I wouldn't miss a chance to hang out with my friends, unlike someone else."

"Is he really not coming?" Riley asked. Still, she didn't want to give up hope.

The librarian called everyone to order and invited the pastor of the local church up to bless the food. "First, we'll eat. In the adjoining room, there are some tables for games and space for dancing. After the meal, the kids have a musical number prepared for us. And word has it, if they sing loudly and gayly enough we might just get a visit from a man in a red suit!"

"Santa Claus!" a kid shouted. Laughter rippled through the crowd.

"Let's have a moment of silence now for the prayer." The paster stood, blessing the food and thanking the community for their generosity.

Dong couldn't focus enough to read. He hadn't been able to since Jing'er had walked into the room. She had been dressed in an A-line black dress, in the 1950s style. She wore four-inch high heels, her long black hair down and ending in large soft curls about her shoulders. Red lips perfected the look. She was dressed to stun.

"What's the occasion?" he had asked.

"It's the town Christmas party. The one that Riley volunteered to help with."

"Oh," Dong said.

"Aren't you coming?" Jing'er said.

"No. I don't attend events anymore." Besides, he was leaving soon. For good.

Jing'er frowned at him. "Maybe I didn't make myself clear. Riley will be there."

"Keep her safe for me." He couldn't think of anyone he could trust more to keep Riley safe.

"Sometimes I have trouble believing you are older than I," Jing'er said. "Well, I am off then. Don't wait up."

"Don't worry, I won't."

Jing'er waved and left. And Dong was left alone in a quiet house. He used to like the quiet, but not anymore. When had that happened?

Riley had brought noise with her, but it was noise that had brought joy to the house. To him. He missed that.

Well, eventually he'd get used to the quiet again, right? No, he probably wouldn't. He'd just learn to live with it.

What would Riley be wearing at the party? If his sister was dressed for the kill, how enticing did Riley look? She would be beautiful. Of that he was certain.

Wait, Jing'er was dressed to the nines. Was she on the hunt? She couldn't harm a human, any more than he could. While he still wasn't sure he wanted to forgive Jing'er, he didn't want her to doom her soul to the abyss. She was still his sister, after all. He had a duty to watch out for her.

He didn't have any special suits for a Christmas party, so his ordinary suit would have to do. He stood up and ran up the stairs to his closet. He had his usual black dress pants on and a white collared shirt with a tie. He pulled out a navy vest and buttoned it on, then picked out his best black suit jacket. It would have to do.

He would keep an eye on Jing'er, for her safety. And he could see Riley as a bonus. Yes, this plan to see Riley—no, to prevent Jing'er from doing something stupid—was a good one.

"For those of you who have finished eating, don't forget there is dancing in the room across the hall," the librarian announced. "In about an hour, we'll invite all the children up to sing and we'll see if we can get Santa to make an appearance."

The crowd cheered.

"This is my cue," Lucas said.

"Is it?" Jing'er said. She smiled, and she wove the thoughts into her magic, *Dance with me, Lucas. You know you want to. You don't even see Riley.*

Lucas beamed at Jing'er. "You do look right beautiful tonight, Jing'er. Save a dance for me. Riley, will you do me the honor of first dance?"

"Uh," Riley said, glancing at Jing'er. Jing'er looked surprised but recovered quickly.

"Of course," Jing'er said.

"Don't tell me you don't want to dance, Riley." Lucas stood up, holding his hand out.

Riley looked back towards the door. "I'm just going—"

Lucas seized her hand and gave a gentle tug. "Come on, sweetheart. I got ya."

Riley allowed herself to be lead, but she cast a glance back at Jing'er and Beatrice.

"That brother of yours is an idiot," Beatrice said to Jing'er, watching Riley walk away.

"On that we can agree. But I don't get it. I was using my charm magic and it didn't seem to affect Lucas. That has never happened."

Beatrice was surprised. "Really?"

Jing'er tapped her chin thoughtfully. "He doesn't seem to be more than human, but there's something unusual about him."

"Riley's monocle!" Beatrice said, standing up.

Jing'er groaned and urged Beatrice to sit back down. "What are you talking about?"

Beatrice's bird tendencies were showing. She nearly flapped her arms around as she talked. "Riley's mother left behind a box of jewelry. But one piece was just a smooth rock about the size of a monocle. Riley can look through it and see someone's true form."

"Box? Was this box about so big?" Jing'er asked, holding her hands out.

Beatrice raised an eyebrow. "Yes."

"I might have seen that box around. Remember that Riley was living with us. I had no idea something like that existed."

"I can't see anything through it, but Riley can. She saw I was a bird."

"I wonder... Maybe we can use it to uncover what sort of vile creature Lucas is."

Beatrice clutched Jing'er arms. "So you think something is off with him too?"

Jing'er gently removed Beatrice's hands. "I know it is. He can resist my charms. That means he has some kind of magic block. He's not wearing anything that I can sense that is causing it, which means it's him. But how... I don't know."

"You keep an eye on Riley," Beatrice said. "I'm going to fly and tell that rotten brother of yours—"

Jing'er held up her hand. "Don't bother. He refused to come."

"I'm not sure about that," Beatrice said suddenly, fluttering her arms excitedly. She pointed behind Jing'er.

Jing'er turned around, and sure enough, she spotted him. In fact, women's heads turned towards him as he entered. Men frowned and scowled. Jing'er beamed. "He's still got that charm." She held up a hand and waved as Dong's eyes locked with hers. He weaved his way through the tables.

"Something's wrong with Lucas," Beatrice blurted out as he arrived at their table.

"What's wrong with him?" Dong asked. He noticed which seat had been Riley's and turned the way she had left.

"She just went to the room across the hall for dancing," Jing'er said. Before she finished, Dong was gone.

Riley was standing against the wall. Lucas was next to her, leaning towards her. Dong frowned. Once again he cursed the rules that prevented him from harming a mortal.

"I'll walk you through it," Lucas was saying. "You just have to trust me."

"It's not that," Riley said. "I've never danced."

"Do you trust me?"

Riley gave a slight nod. Almost hesitant.

"I promise you, if you follow my lead, you'll be fine."

"I think I'll watch for a bit longer," Riley said. She glanced up at the dance floor and her eyes landed on Dong, causing a smile to appear on her face.

Lucas followed Riley's gaze. Lucas did not look happy to see him.

Dong couldn't help it, he smiled back at Riley as he approached. "Riley," he said.

"You came," Riley said, a skip to her step as she moved towards him. "You really came."

"I had it on good authority that you'd be here," Dong said. "Will you dance with me?"

Riley nodded and accepted his offered hand.

Lucas frowned and reached for Riley's hand. "She's my date."

Dong's hand closed on Riley's, fingers interlaced, having her step behind him. "I wasn't aware this was a date." He looked at Riley and raised an eyebrow.

"It's not," Riley said. "I came with Beatrice."

Lucas threw up his hands. "I can tell when I'm not wanted. But, don't forget who's driving you home, Riley. Be good and save a dance for me." He took up her other hand and kissed it. Riley quickly pulled it back.

Dong turned and escorted Riley to the dance floor, turning to face her. "Did I hear correctly that you've never danced?"

Riley nodded. "I haven't. For one thing, no one ever asked me."

Dong's lips quirked up in another smile. "Lucas asked you."

Riley shook her head. "He dragged me. I also didn't dance with him." Her eyes were sparkling as she looked into Dong's eyes.

Pulling her closer, Dong placed her free hand on his shoulder, and his at the small of her back. "You can place your other hand on my shoulder too, but you'll need to let go of my hand for that."

"Oh," Riley said. She freed his hand and put her hand on Dong's shoulder.

Dong smiled and placed his second hand behind her back. She was now firmly in his arms. "The simplest dance, and one I'll only ever dance with you, is this." He started to sway back and forth, slowly, despite the faster tempo of the music.

Riley looked around the room. An older couple was moving similar to them, slowly swaying together, but the majority was keeping pace with the faster holiday beat.

"Riley," Dong said, drawing her attention back to him. She turned to look up at him and Dong realized he could get lost in her eyes. "Ignore everyone else. It's just you and me."

Riley nodded, before looking down at their feet.

"Let me take you home tonight," Dong said.

"What?" Riley looked back up, her cheeks coloring.

Dong shook his head. "I don't want you letting that man take you anywhere. Let me take you home."

"What about Beatrice?"

"She'll be fine," he said.

Riley focused on his neck and picked at the back of his collar. "I can't just leave her."

"Jing'er will be with her."

Riley seemed to consider that.

Dong hesitated only a moment. "What is that man to you?"

Riley blinked up at him, curious. "What man?"

Dong nodded towards the wall where Lucas was talking with another woman.

Riley glanced over, then back at Dong, a smile springing up on her face. "Are you jealous?"

Dong coughed, looking away.

"Oh my gosh, I think you are." Riley was obviously happy about something.

Dong frowned. "I just don't like him."

Riley sighed. "It seems none of my friends do, although I can't see why. Lucas seems like a good guy to me. He's helped me quite a few times, and I consider him a—"

Dong was trying to be patient and listen, but darn it all, he just wanted Riley to stop talking about that imbecile. He watched her lips move as she talked, and before he knew what possessed him, he kissed her.

Riley's eyes flew wide, then she was kissing him back.

A moment later, someone thumped hard on Dong's shoulder. When he broke the kiss to turn that way, a fist hit him.

"That's my girl you're kissing. Don't forget you dumped her!"

Dancing couples scattered.

Riley's arms shot out to the side as she moved between Dong and Lucas.

"Don't," she said, squaring Lucas down. "Shame on you, Lucas."

Riley turned to Dong. "Let's go." She glared at Lucas again, which thrilled Dong.

Rubbing his jaw, Dong nodded. They left the dance room and entered the adjacent room that had been for dining. A group of kids started to sing jubilantly. Jingle bells were being shaken as Riley lead them to the table where Jing'er and Beatrice were talking.

"Bea, Dong has offered to drive us home."

Beatrice looked up and noticed the dark expression on Dong's face.

"I'll take you home, Beatrice," Jing'er said. "Stay with me for Santa's arrival. I want to see Santa Claus."

"You do realize it's just a man dressed up in a suit?" Beatrice said.

"It's not really Santa Claus?" Jing'er asked. "Shh! Don't spoil my fun" Jing'er winked and shifted form to a little girl.

"Careful, Jing'er," Dong said.

"I got it. Don't worry. I made sure to cast a quick shielding spell. No one saw."

Dong shook his head.

Beatrice frowned at Jing'er. "Great, now I'm babysitting."

It was Jing'er's turn to pout. "I don't need a babysitter, but I plan to make a Christmas wish."

"Be good, you two," Riley said. "I'm getting Dong home before Lucas decides to deck him again."

Jing'er and Beatrice turned to them. "What?!"

Riley shook her head. "I'll tell you about it later." She then pulled on her coat and looped her arm through Dong's.

As they headed towards the exit, Lucas chased after them. "Riley! Wait! Let me explain."

Without a second thought, Dong angled his right hand and shot a burst of magic at Lucas, knocking him backwards. Lucas braced himself and recovered quickly. Riley ignored his plea, tightening her grip on Dong's arm.

"Let's go home," she said. "But first, could you do some hocus pocus so that everyone else forgets the punch?"

Dong searched her eyes and nodded. "If you want me to." He let go of her arm long enough to weave an intricate pattern of magic. Riley thought she saw a glimmer in his hands for a brief moment, but dismissed it as a trick of the eye.

"Lucas makes me soo angry. I hope he gets stuck in a snowstorm on the way home." As she said it, snow started to fall. "But only him. I don't wish a storm on the townspeople." The snow swirled about, little bursts of wind tugging at Riley's coat as if to answer her.

"Come with me," Dong said. He took Riley's hand and portaled Riley home.

Chapter 24

Dong was pacing in his library when Jing'er arrived home. She was back to her normal form.

"Did you enjoy yourself?" he asked.

Jing'er grinned, inordinately happy. "I did. I sat on Santa's lap and asked him if he could make my brother sensible." She laughed.

Dong scowled. He was being sensible. He was the only one of them taking the problem seriously. And—

147

Jing'er held up her hands. "I'm teasing. But the transformation took more out of me than I thought. I had forgotten how hard it is to maintain it for more than a few minutes."

"We have a problem," Dong said.

Jing'er took a seat. "Which is what?"

"Riley," he said.

Jing'er scoffed and eyed her brother. "I don't think Riley's the problem."

Dong sighed. "No, she isn't, but keeping her safe *is*."

"Have her move back in," Jing'er said, as if it was that simple.

"I kissed her." Dong ran his hands through his hair, resuming his pacing. "I couldn't help it. I can't have her living here until I can get a grip on my feelings for her."

"There's a simple solution, brother."

Dong shook his head. He loosened his tie and sat down. "I doubt that." He felt weary.

Jing'er placed a hand on his arm. It gave him the feeling that her question was important. "Have you considered surrendering to those feelings? For many, love only comes once."

"No."

Jing'er shifted away from him. "If you can't come to believe that joy will far outweigh the risk of harm, then you might as well let another man marry her. You should encourage it. That Lucas seems to like her."

Dong's growl had a dangerous edge to it. He got up and resumed his pacing.

Jing'er continued. "My charms don't seem to work on him. I don't know if it's because he has a red string of fate with Riley, or if he is somehow managing to block my magic."

Dong stopped and turned to face his sister.

"Is that possible?"

"Which part?" Jing'er said.

"The part about blocking your magic," Dong said impatiently.

Jing'er shrugged. "That's the only thing I can make out. I suppose a red string of fate could block my charms though. That's a God-ordained match, after all."

Dong's emotions flared. "I *am* bound to Riley with a red string of fate."

"And don't forget that," Jing'er said. "I don't understand why you fight it so. But it brings me to my other point, something isn't to be trusted about that Lucas."

Dong nodded. "We'll have to keep an eye on him for now. Is there any magical trinket that can block seduction magic?"

Jing'er shrugged. "Maybe there was once. But it would give off some energy. Your cultivation is higher than mine, have you sensed anything?"

Dong shook his head. "Nothing." He had attributed his dislike of Lucas to the man's interest in Riley. Could there be something more to it?

Jing'er turned and looked out the window. "It's snowing heavily. There seems to be magic in the storm. Did you do anything?

Dong took a seat. "Other than bid a large a group of people to not remember that Lucas struck me, no."

Jing'er faced him. "Why did Lucas hit you?"

Dong grunted. "I kissed Riley. I thought I told you that."

"Why would Lucas hit you about that? It's not like Riley is dating him."

"Does he know that?" Dong asked.

"She doesn't even like him that way," Jing'er added.

"Again, does he know that?" Dong pulled at his hair. "Arggh. This is driving me crazy."

"Dong, dear brother, let's ask Riley to move back in."

Dong sighed and stood up. "We'll discuss this later. I'm going to bed, I'll see you in the morning."

"Good night," Jing'er said. It was only after he had left and fallen asleep that she remembered that she wanted to ask about what had been in Riley's stolen box.

Riley was making hot chocolate when Beatrice returned home. True to her word, Jing'er had seen her home, for which Riley was grateful.

"Is that fox here?" Beatrice asked.

"No, he went home after he dropped me off." Riley poured some cocoa into a mug. "Did you want some?"

"Sure. The storm is picking up out there and it's really cold," Beatrice said, accepting the mug. "Thank you."

"I guess the weather was wrong. It was supposed to be clear tonight."

"Weather can change," Beatrice said. "The gods can be fickle."

Riley went to look out the window. "Do you think they are causing the storm?"

Beatrice shrugged. "Who knows. They really aren't supposed to mess with the mortal world. But I do sense some magic in the air."

Riley smiled, her face lighting up. "Maybe it's Christmas magic. Santa comes tomorrow night."

"That would make the magic tomorrow night, not tonight."

Riley grabbed her mug and took a seat on the couch. "But there was magic tonight. Such magic." She smiled dreamily.

"Really?"

Riley nodded. "I'll tell you a secret." She leaned forward, eyes twinkling. "Dong kissed me when we were dancing."

"You danced with him? What happened to dancing with Lucas?"

Riley gave Beatrice an imploring look. "Don't spoil my mood by bringing him up. I get mad just thinking about it."

"Ah, okay," Beatrice said. "I won't bring him up. So, tell me more about this kiss."

Riley's face lit up as she began describing how Dong positioned them for the dance, having Beatrice fill in for herself as she demonstrated. "It was like this. He had his arms about my waist, we were staring into each other eyes, and then he kissed me!" Riley put her hands up by her mouth and squealed.

"For his cold insistence about not being with you, he sure is kissing you a great deal."

"I hope he kisses me again," Riley said. She finished her cocoa and yawned. "I'm going to head to bed."

"Huh huh," Beatrice said. "I'm sure you'll have sweet dreams about a certain fox." That got a happy giggle from Riley and Beatrice shuddered. In bird, she trilled, "I don't know what she sees in that man."

Late that night, when it was very early in the morning, a text message beeped on Riley's phone. For her part, she slept through it. Dreaming of her and Dong.

Call me when you get this. Did you get home safe? The snow made the roads terrible. I just got in. I'm worried about you.

Chapter 25

Riley was still riding cloud nine when she joined Beatrice at the table for breakfast. "You must have slept well," Beatrice said, setting a plate of pancakes on the table.

"I did. In fact, it was smelling the food that woke me up." Riley pulled out her chair and took a seat, her eyes finally landing on the two extra plates at the table. "Are we having company?"

"Now you notice," Beatrice said. In a loud stage whisper, she added, "They are in the kitchen right now. Jing'er and I wouldn't let *him* wake you up."

Jing'er came out of the kitchen carrying a platter of scrambled eggs. "I made the eggs. I had Dong cut up some fruit."

Dong followed with a large bowl of fruit.

Jing'er set the platter down. "We also made him set the table and do other menial tasks to keep him busy."

"You didn't?" Riley gasped. Turning to Dong she beamed. "Good morning!"

Dong smiled back. "Good morning."

Riley put her hands to either side of her face and said, "I must still be dreaming." She patted her cheeks and blinked, wide-eyed.

Dong pulled out the chair next to her. "You aren't dreaming." He leaned over and kissed the top of her head as he took his seat.

Jing'er cleared her throat and Beatrice threw a waded-up napkin at him. Dong flicked a finger at Beatrice and the napkin whipped back at her.

"That's cheating," Beatrice said.

"What is?" Dong focused on taking a couple of pancakes and placing them on Riley's plate.

Riley looked at Beatrice. "Did I forget to wake up?" she mouthed.

"It really snowed out," Jing'er said. "There's like a foot of that hideous white stuff."

"I like snow," Riley said, turning to look at Dong. Should she pinch herself?

154

"It looks quite lovely out," Dong said. "I was hoping you'd want to go to the woods with me today and enjoy the scenery."

Riley nodded. She took several bites of food before the tears started.

"What's wrong?" Beatrice asked.

Riley quickly wiped her eyes. "It's just that no one has ever spent the Christmas holidays with me since my parents died. And today, I get to spend it with my friends—my family."

Jing'er sat up straighter. "Do you hear that, brother? I *am* included in this family of misfits."

"I found Riley first," Beatrice said.

Riley laughed. "You did." She turned to glance at Dong. He was overly focused on cutting a bit of pancake. A smile spread on Riley's face. "If this is a dream, I hope I never wake up."

The four of them finished eating breakfast, enjoying their time together at the table. After they cleaned up, Riley put on her winter coat and boots. She grabbed her phone and stopped. "Oh, I have a message and some missed calls. Give me a second to answer this." She hit some buttons and hit send. A moment later her phone rang.

"Hi, Lucas." She paused, listening. "Yes, I got home safe. That's why I texted you back. You said you were worried."

Jing'er glanced at Dong. Dong was looking at the floor, but Jing'er was sure he was using his acute hearing.

"Can I call you back later? I'm about to go out. No. I can't. I'm spending the day with my family. Okay. Merry

Christmas. Bye." Riley ended the call and started to put her phone in her pocket, but changed her mind. She powered it off and put it down on the end table by the couch. "I don't need it."

"You might want to have it on you," Dong said. "It's a safety thing these days."

Riley shook her head. "Nah. I have you with me."

Dong smiled, accepting her answer. "Shall we go?" He waved his arms in the intricate pattern Riley had seen before, then taking her hand they stepped through.

Riley looked around. The snow was undisturbed here. Small lights hovered and danced over the trees, mimicking Christmas lights. Old fashioned lanterns were hung, leading away down a path.

"It's beautiful," Riley said. She slowly moved in a circle, taking it all in

"It is. I wanted to do something special," Dong said. "We went through a lot of trouble for today."

Riley came full circle and stopped, facing Dong. "Did you and Jing'er do this all for me?"

"Who else would it be for?" Dong said. "Jing'er told me that Christmas was your favorite holiday because it was special for you and your mother."

"It was," Riley said.

Dong took her hand. "Tell me about her, your mother."

"I'm not sure where to start," Riley said. "I was very young when my parents died. I mostly remember looking at Christmas lights and singing carols together. Her singing to me at bedtime."

"Do you have a favorite song she sang?" Dong asked.

Riley nodded. "There was this one. It asked that I be blessed with love and health and that I'm given time to enjoy them. It also had a line about angels guarding over me. My mother believed in angels."

"Do you believe in angels?"

Riley thought for a moment. "Yeah, I do. Maybe not the conventional kind with feathery wings." She shrugged. "Here's the million-dollar question. Do you believe in angels?"

Dong looked up at the sky. Snow started to fall. "I am starting to believe. You are an angel."

Riley nudged his arm. "No I'm not, but I like what you did there."

Dong grinned.

"Have you ever tried to catch snow on your tongue?" Riley closed her eyes and stuck out her tongue.

"What?" Dong said. "You're serious."

Riley opened her eyes and looked at Dong. With her tongue still out she said, "Try it." She lifted her chin a couple of times, eying him.

Dong closed his eyes and stuck out his tongue. "Like this?"

"Yes," Riley said. She closed her eyes and waited patiently. After a few minutes, she said, "I got one! Did you get any?"

"No," Dong said. "This is rather silly."

"Keep trying."

Dong closed his eyes again and stuck out his tongue. Riley laughed to herself and reached down for some clean white show. In the next instant, a burst of cold splattered on Dong's face and tongue.

"See, you did it!" Riley said, clapping and laughing.

Dong wiped the snow from his face. "Huh-huh," he said. He pointed to the ground and with a flick of his wrist pointed at Riley. Several snowballs formed and flew at her. She attempted to dodge.

"Hey, that's cheating!"

"Really?" Dong said, sending several more at her, but missing her on purpose. "What about your sneak attack?"

Riley put her hands on her hips. "What sneak attack? I just helped and upped your chances of catching snow."

"I see," Dong said, breaking into a run towards her.

Riley shrieked and took off. Dong let her have the lead for a while, then he pounced, grabbing her around the waist. The momentum had them spin, and she lost balance. Dong pivoted so that when they landed, Riley was on top and unharmed. She stared into his eyes. They smiled at each other, lost in the moment. Dong's eyes moved to her lips. Riley's cheeks flushed and she quickly got up.

As Riley dusted the snow off her pants, Dong sat up. The lights upon the trees danced, coming closer, circling about them. Riley held out her palm, and they danced above her hand. "I am really dreaming."

"Riley," Dong said, pulling her attention back to him. "If this is a dream, then I am dreaming too. Let's not wake up." He wanted that dream, where he didn't have to worry about draining her life force. Where he could be with her, forever. His love for her wasn't going to end. Maybe Jing'er was right. He should just surrender to it. Love her the best he could.

"What are these?" Riley said. She turned back to the dancing lights.

"Those are fairy lights," Dong said. "Do you like them?"

Riley nodded. "I feel like my life has become magical with you." She turned to face him. "I love you."

Something inside of Dong broke loose, and his wall came down. "I love you, too. I've loved you from the moment I met you. I want to marry you and only you. I wish to be with you now and always. Darn it all, I can't—"

"Shhh," Riley said, kneeling in front of him and covering his mouth with her mittened hand. "If that is a proposal, then I accept. I claim you. I claim you now and forever." She held out her hand.

Dong wasn't wearing gloves. When their hands clasped, a red light appeared, wrapping around them, before vanishing, leaving a red ring upon Dong's hand.

"What's this?" Riley whispered for she felt a ring on her hand under her glove.

"I'm surrendering," Dong said. He gave a quick tug and Riley fell into his arms. "I'm surrendering to my wife."

Chapter 26

Dong and Riley arrived at the end of the wintery path. "This is my home," Dong said.

"This doesn't look like Fox Hill."

Dong touched the lock on the gate and pushed open the door. "Not that home. This is what I want to show you today."

"Oh," Riley said, following him inside. It was an open courtyard. Lanterns and red ribbons and flowers adorned

the trees and building. To the right was an iced-over pond with a weeping willow standing guardian. Just behind the tree, was the first of several buildings.

"This first building is the servant's room. It's so they are closest to the door."

"Is there anyone here now?" Riley asked. Everything looked well cared for. A path had even been cleared in the snow. "It looks decorated for a party."

Dong looked at Riley. "No one comes here anymore. Not for a couple of hundred years."

"It's in really good condition," Riley said.

Dong smiled sadly. "It's preserved by magic. "

"I see," Riley said. She opened the door to the servant's room. It looked comfortable. It was an open space, with six beds. There were two wardrobes, one bureau, and a shelf. On the shelf was a porcelain vase and some books. She paused at the books.

"Come this way," Dong said.

Riley followed.

"My room was this way."

Riley turned a circle, taking in her surroundings as they walked. "Why don't you stay here? This place is lovely." Indeed it was, and Dong seemed to belong here, more than he had in her world. His old-fashioned yet modern-style clothing may be out of place in a yard that looked like it belonged in ancient China, but Riley couldn't shake the feeling that this place felt like he was home to her. He belonged here. She could belong here.

Dong's voice brought her out of her reverie. "I had this house built for when Jinxia and I married. What you see are the decorations for what would have been our wedding."

"Oh," Riley said. "Maybe it's not that lovely after all."

Dong grinned. "Are you jealous?"

"A little," Riley grumbled.

Dong tugged her closer and put his arm around her shoulder.

Riley looked up at him. "Were you mean to her, too?"

Dong blinked. "Me, mean? Never."

Riley shoved him away, but Dong kept his arm around her. He kissed the top of her head. "I am truly sorry for how I treated you."

"You better be," Riley said.

"To answer your question," Dong said, opening the door to a larger dwelling. "Yes, I was mean to her. I lead her to her death."

"Jing'er told me what happened. It wasn't your fault, you do realize that?"

Dong's answer was to squeeze Riley's hand.

Riley followed Dong and stepped into the room. The bed had a red fabric curtain, tied by large red ribbons. "You really went all out."

"We never did get married," Dong said. "Not really."

"Why do you refer to her as your wife then?"

"Back then, when the marriage agreement was made, it was official. We had started the marriage rites, but never completed them."

Riley walked over to the bed and took off her glove and touched the curtain, followed by the red blanket. "Silk?"

Dong nodded. He walked over to the wardrobe and opened it. Two garments of red silk and green outer robes were inside. Dong pulled out a pretty gown. "This was the bridal gown," Dong said. "And this one was for me." Riley noticed the blood and torn fabric.

"So it happened on your wedding day," Riley said. "The tragic events."

Dong nodded, going to sit on the bed.

"Why didn't she just cry off? Although, I bet I know why. It's because she really did love you and hoped her plan to be with you worked."

"Do you think so?" Dong hadn't been sure, and for years that doubt ate at him.

Riley gave a firm nod, joining Dong where he sat. "How can she not have?"

Dong laid back, staring up at the ceiling. "For many years I didn't believe she had loved me."

Riley also laid back but rolled on her side to look at Dong. "I think that is understandable."

"I also realized, I didn't know what love really was and could be until you came into my life."

Riley turned and held up her hand, the red ring sparkling in the light. "Did the ring you gave Jinxia magically appear like this one?"

Dong sat up and looked at his hand. "No. That one I gave her was meant to protect her. I gave it to her just before we were to wed. I pledged an oath that should she die, I would die with her. I meant it to show that I loved her and wouldn't make her a dead bride. Although I agreed to her father's terms of our marriage."

"His terms were too harsh," Riley said.

Dong turned to face Riley. "You are remarkable," he said.

"Show me how remarkable," Riley said, tugging Dong closer to her.

"Amazingly remarkable. I don't understand how you put up with me."

"Me either," Riley said. "Must be love."

Riley was sleeping peacefully, but Dong wasn't. He was thinking. They had talked for a while before Riley looked really tired, so he touched her face, smoothing the hair from her brow while he nudged her to sleep. He then pulled the blanket over her, making sure she was snug and all covered up. He then laid down next to her, on top of the remaining blanket. He sent a missive to Jing'er so that she wouldn't worry and come looking for them. Riley was safe; they would return in the morning.

The intricate red ring they both now wore must be from the red string of fate, and because of it, they were married. At least, in his world. What were the customs in Riley's world? He studied her face, tracing her nose and feeling for her reassuring gentle breathing.

Riley was a gift from heaven. Of that he was certain. He'd have to thank the empress for tying them together so that they would meet, and so that Riley wouldn't give up on a fool such as him. He kissed her forehead.

He had kissed her multiple times now, and he realized, that not since their first kiss had he not been able to control his desire for her inner energy. It gave him hope that he could cultivate the self-control to not devour her. Maybe, someday, they could even have children together. He smiled, imagining little Riley's running around. It was with these images dancing in his mind that he fell asleep himself.

Chapter 27

Dong was adjusting his shirt cuff when Jing'er walked in the door. "Don't you knock?" he asked.

"We were worried," Jing'er said, as a little bird flew into the room and transformed in a puff of blue sparkles,

"Where's Riley?" Beatrice asked.

Dong nodded towards the bed. Riley, now awake, buried herself deeper into the blanket. Beatrice rushed over to her.

Jing'er raised an eyebrow and took her brother's hand.

"A magic ring?" It was a dark red ring, with gold pin-stripes framing each side. The band of red, glittered as if pieces of stars were captured inside. She glanced back at Riley, who wore the same ring on her hand that was peeking out from the blanket. "Did you finally propose marriage? Do what can't be undone? Here I was worried for nothing."

Dong shook his head. "I wasn't planning on it."

Jing'er frowned, looking about the room that was decorated for a wedding. "I don't quite understand."

Riley sat up. "It was spur of the moment."

Beatrice finally noticed the wedding decor. "I would say so," she muttered. "The fox is a sly one."

Riley swung her feet out of the bed, dropped the blanket, and went over to stand by Dong. "This was from Dong's wedding to Jinxia. We talked about a lot of things last night."

Dong put his arm around Riley and faced his sister. "Jing'er, sister, meet your sister-in-law."

Jing'er looked from Dong to Riley. Riley turned scarlet. Raising an eyebrow, Jing'er studied her brother. "You're not tricking me?"

"Riley claimed me. And somehow..." He held up his hand, showing the ring. "Riley's my wife. We just need to formally register it."

"Not so fast, brother. We need to plan a wedding, and none of this leftover wedding stuff," Jing'er said, waving her arms about. "Riley deserves it. She's putting up with you after all." Jing'er put her arm around Riley and tugged her away from Dong. "I knew he would come to his senses."

"I feel like I'm dreaming," Riley said. She turned back to Dong. "You aren't just going to disappear on me, are you?"

Dong smiled and held up his hand, displaying the ring. "You claimed me, and I—" His smile faltered a little when he noticed the ring on Riley's finger fading slightly. Something wasn't right. Fortunately, she didn't seem to notice.

"Ok," she said. "You promised. I'm your wife now, so it's official." The way she said 'official' made Dong smile.

"Yes, Riley," Dong said. "My wife."

"Let's go look at wedding gowns," Jing'er said.

"It's Christmas Day, no store is open. Besides, I want—" Riley's voice was suddenly gone as Jing'er teleported them out.

Dong watched his sister and *his* woman leave, before allowing his smile to completely fade. Riley's ring fading worried him more than he cared to admit. He had seen the red string of fate appear and bind them together. While it was true that Empress had bound them with it, Riley had had the ultimate choice to be with him or not. On top of that, she had somehow invoked a magical claim to him. How? And why did the ring then fade?

"Beatrice, I need you to do something for me."

"Okay," Beatrice said. She tossed some of her long hair back over her shoulder.

"Go to the Heavenly Library and ask the Lore Keeper to prepare a list of all the books on the red string of fate."

"The red string of fate. Got it."

Dong watched as Beatrice left on her errand, then he followed the way Jing'er and Riley had gone.

Chapter 28

Dong threw the book to the floor. "There's nothing useful here either!"

The Lore Keeper, in his long robes of pale blue and white, bent down and picked up the tome, inspecting it to make sure it was intact.

"Abusing the books won't help," he said. He placed the book on a shelf, waved his hand, and with a flash of light, the book vanished and appeared upon a spot up high on

the shelves. The shelves were high and never quite ending. There were many books the lore keeper was entrusted with.

Dong wearily looked up towards the high ceiling. "My Riley would be enchanted by your book collection."

The Lore Keeper smiled and picked up a wooden scroll. "I would like to meet this remarkable woman who tamed the untamable fox. The youngest Star Keeper thought it wasn't possible even with the red string of fate. She now gets to clean the library for a year. She should be here soon, as the day begins."

"You've been placing bets on me, I see."

"One could say that," the keeper said. He tapped the scroll in his hands thoughtfully. "Perhaps you are seeking an answer to the wrong question."

Dong frowned. What did that mean?

"The ring is an enchantment. Love is, perhaps, the greatest of all enchantments. How Riley made it, who knows? Maybe it lies in who she is."

"But she is mortal," Dong said. "Mortals don't have magic." Dong picked up another book. "So the answer must be in the red string of fate."

"Is she?" The lore keeper sighed and placed the wooden scroll down. "You can keep looking at things that way, and you might find the answer you seek. Or you won't."

Dong thought a moment. "Are all those born in the mortal realm truly mortal?"

"Their souls are immortal, but they are not immortals, nor are they necessarily *not* immortals either."

Dong flipped through several more pages. He was getting nowhere. The lore keeper was talking in circles.

"Another immortal was also recently looking for answers to a riddle that perplexed him. I gave the same advice I give to you now. Not all creatures of the mortal realm are born of mortals. Not all immortals who dwell there are living a mortal life."

Dong looked up. "Are you speaking of the fae?"

The lore keeper stroked his beard thoughtfully. "Both them and the many others. You know all *you* need to know about the string of fate. The ring you wear is a token of the strongest power, and only one can make it."

"Riley," Dong said. "She can make it."

The Lore Keeper smiled. "You are learning."

"We just circled back to the beginning. Riley's fate was bound to cross and walk alongside mine. She chose to love me and in turn claimed my heart. But then the red string of fate became a ring and I saw it fade! I can't lose her."

"The ring is called the Stardust ring," a woman's voice said.

"Ah, the star keeper has come to clean." The Lore Keeper patted the scroll again and gave Dong a pointed look. "Sometimes the answers are right in front of you. If you'll excuse me, I shall leave first."

Dong and the Star Keeper bowed in farewell.

"What do you know of the Stardust ring," Dong asked, turning to the Star Keeper.

The Star Keeper was one of the lesser gods under the Star Goddess. As she was young, her hair was still dark, unlike the white of the Lore Keeper's hair. She handed

Dong a rag. "If you will clean this hall for me for a month, I will tell you."

Dong wanted to refuse, but his patience was running thin and he was desperate. "Deal, although I fear I have the short end of the stick."

"Let's make a contract." She held out her hand and a piece of paper appeared. She handed it to Dong. "Write down, 'I, Dong of the Fox Clan, hereby agree to clean the library on behalf of Mei-Xing of the Sky Clan for one month.'"

Dong wrote it and signed it, sealing it with his thumbprint.

Mei-Xing grinned as she rolled up the agreement and stuck it into her sleeve, where it vanished. "Only a high immortal can make a stardust ring. It's made from the tears of stars."

"But Riley isn't an immortal."

The little goddess shrugged. "The other night the stars in the west wept. The High Goddess said it meant one of the Hidden Ones had—"

"What does that have to do with Riley?" Dong interrupted. Heaven help him, if he was tricked he'd make this little goddess pay him back tenfold.

She shrugged. "The stardust will become a ring. Each stardust ring has one match, for the Hidden One's only love once eternally."

Dong realized Mei-Xing might be on to something. "I see. What would cause such a ring to fade?" His more pressing question though was, would the mortal who wore the ring survive its fading?

The goddess handed Dong a rag for dusting. "That I don't know. And now I'm going to go play."

"Mei-Xing," Dong called after her.

She paused at the door. "If I think of anything else, I will be sure to tell you. And thank you for helping me with cleaning. The Lore Keeper tricked me, after all." And with that, she was gone.

Dong took the rag and started removing scrolls and dusting. When he got to the one that the Lore Keeper had left stuck out he paused. The Lore Keeper had said that he was asking the wrong questions. Mei-Xing had mentioned the stars wept and a stardust ring was created, and only Hidden Ones could craft it, and only once. Riley had claimed him and the rings now adorned their fingers. It may have had nothing to do with the red string of fate then.

Was Riley what they called a Hidden One? What exactly did that mean for her? And what did the ring fading mean? It certainly could not be good. Dong put the rag down, put the scroll into his suit coat's inner pocket, and turned to leave the library. When he tried to walk through the door, an invisible force pushed him back. He frowned and tried to teleport out. He started to port, then found himself walking right back into the library. He cursed. Well, if he could not leave until he was done, he would use magic to clean the library. He waved his hand and sent a magical blast towards the shelves. Nothing happened. He tried again and again. Darn it all, he was going to be stuck actually dusting the shelves and books for that Mei-Xing. Well, he better get to it then so he could get back to Riley.

The Lore Keeper found him there when he returned later that evening. The old man chuckled. "Mei-Xing traded for knowledge? I hope it was a good trade for you. How long did she rope you in for?"

"A month." Dong looked around and frowned. "And magic doesn't work."

The Lore Keeper shook his head. "Of course not. Magic doesn't and shouldn't work for chores. It is important that immortals and fae learn the value of hard work. Not all of them chose to experience mortality, but all need to learn to better themselves. To cultivate a higher character."

"And now I have to—is there a way out of the contract?"

Dong knew the answer before he asked. There wouldn't be unless Mei-Xing agreed. And oftentimes, bargaining your way out dug you deeper in instead.

"I'm afraid not," the lore keeper said. "But, each night I alone can let you leave upon completion of that day's chores. I will assign one of my assistants to help you, and you can leave here sooner than the close of day in the mortal realm. The sun will have to have begun its descent. It is the best I can do."

"A full day?" Dong ran his hand through his hair.

"It is the best I can do, given that Mei-Xing's shift is in the day. At night she has her duties."

"I thank you for that," Dong said. "I guess I will see you tomorrow morning."

The Lore keeper smiled. "I will be waiting. Perhaps we can talk about what you discover."

Dong nodded and walked out of the library. He needed to get home. He needed to see Riley.

Chapter 29

I n his slow and flirtatious way, Lucas smiled. He knew his charismatic smile was alluring to the ladies, and he wanted to charm the one in front of him.

Riley was carrying a moving box to her car. She, however impossible that was, was immune to his charms.

Riley put the box in the truck and closed the door. She turned to face Lucas. "I'm not going to be a housekeeper. I'm going to be his wife."

Lucas snorted. "You've said that. But why would you marry someone like him? He tossed you out not what, two months ago? He only just showed up. What is wrong with you?"

"Lucas, I would like to remain on friendly terms with you but I can't if you are going to be like this."

Lucas held up his hands in defeat. "Okay. But you'll tell me if you run into any problems? Wait, you aren't in trouble, are you? There are better ways to handle a-you-know-what without running into a marriage."

Beatrice came out of the apartment with another box, which she placed in the backseat of Riley's car. "I think that's the last one for this load. I wonder what has kept Dong?" She shrugged. "I'll go lock up so we can take this over to the house."

Riley turned to look at Lucas. "What are you talking about?"

"Girls usually keep track of this sort of thing, but you're not late on something?" Lucas made a show of counting on his fingers.

"I'm late getting these *home*. The sun is already setting." She indicated the sky.

"I'm not talking about that kind of late," Lucas said. He patted his stomach and eyed hers, raising his eyebrow. "Huh?"

"What?" Seeming to finally understand, she colored in embarrassment. "Not that it's any of your business." She pulled open the car door and climbed in.

Beatrice got in the passenger said, shut the door, and asked, "What's not anyone's business? And by anyone, I mean his." She nodded towards Lucas.

"Did you hear what he asked me?" She frowned as put on her seatbelt.

Beatrice strapped on her belt. "What?"

"I think he asked if I was pregnant."

Beatrice made some noises that could only be called a squawk.

Riley started up the engine and pulled away. "I can't believe that idiot. I'm not that kind of girl."

"Mmmhmmm," Beatrice said.

Riley eyed Beatrice. "What does that mean?"

Beatrice tapped her knees. "You did spend the night together. With Dong."

"I did no such thing!"

Beatrice wanted to make a point, even if she was teasing her friend. "What do you call it when you stayed out all night at his old place?"

"But we didn't do anything of *that* sort," Riley said. "We just talked. Dong was the perfect gentleman. Besides, he didn't even get under the covers with me."

Beatrice nodded. "You know that. I know that. But Lucas doesn't, and he's interested in you."

Riley took her head, stopping at a light. "I have told him in no uncertain terms that we'll never be more than friends, even before becoming Dong's wife."

"Yeah, well you aren't exactly Dong's wife yet."

Riley waved her left hand in front of Beatrice's nose.

Beatrice let out a puff of air. "I just mean I don't think Lucas is the sort to give up easily."

"I wish he would. I will only ever love Dong. If he wanted to take our marriage to the next level—" Riley grew silent, her cheeks coloring.

Beatrice started giggling.

"I'm being serious," Riley said.

"You can't even say it," Beatrice said, then added something in bird.

"That doesn't mean I'm not willing to... you know."

"Have you thought about when you'd actually like to have the wedding?" Beatrice asked.

The light turned green, so Riley resumed driving. "Not really. When the ring appeared, I felt like something special happened. Something that tied us more than a wedding certificate ever could. I felt it in my soul."

"I think you might be confusing indigestion," Beatrice teased.

"No," Riley said. "It was—I can't describe it. Like the very stars themselves gave us their blessing."

"You've got it bad. Now while I agree that Dong is very handsome, his personality needs work."

Riley grinned. "Hey! That's my Dong you're insulting."

They laughed and talked the rest of the way to Fox Hill. As they were pulling in, Beatrice said, "You know, you could ask to get married at Celestial Ridge with the Empress and Emperor standing in for both of your parents. I mean, they did help bring you together."

Riley turned off the engine. "You think so?"

Jing'er, who had heard the car engine approaching was waiting for them outside.

Beatrice nodded, opening her door. "Even mortals have to acknowledge a marriage witnessed by the gods."

"What's this about mortals and gods?" Jing'er asked as Riley opened her door.

Riley shut her door and turned to Jing'er. "Beatrice was saying Dong and I should ask the Celestial Emperor and Empress to witness our wedding in lieu of our parents."

"And that horrible Lucas will have to acknowledge it because even mortals have to acknowledge such a union," Beatrice finished.

Jing'er broke into a grin. "I think that is a smashing idea. I'm sure my brother will go for it. You can have a traditional wedding, red dress and all like you told me you want, and then a white gown and tuxedo reception here at Fox Hill."

"I don't need a reception," Riley said. "I don't have anybody I want to invite other than you guys."

"Aww, isn't that sweet." Jing'er put her arm around Riley's shoulders, leading her into the house, the boxes in the car forgotten. "We need to invite your aunt and cousin so we can rub it into their noses how well off you are marrying, and we need to make sure Lucas knows you are off the market because he's too stupid to accept it."

"Don't remind me about him. Did you know he had the audacity to ask me if I was..." Riley made a round motion over her stomach.

"Getting fat?" Jing'er asked, winking at Riley.

"Pregnant," Beatrice said. Riley cringed with how loud her statement seemed to be.

"Who is what?" Dong asked, walking in from his library.

Jing'er turned to face him, putting a hand on her hip. "Oh, *now* you're home?" She waved towards the front door. "Be a dear and get Riley's boxes out of her car."

"Boxes?" Dong walked to the door and looked outside.

Jing'er looked thoughtful. "Did I forget to tell you? While you've been working that day *job*, I asked Riley to move in. Her bedroom furniture arrived today."

"Why would she need her own bedroom?" Dong asked, as he walked outside and brought in all the boxes in one armload. With a flick of magic, the doors could be heard closing behind him. He set the boxes down near the stairs.

Jing'er shook her head and gave Riley a sympathetic look. "That boy. You can't stay in his room yet. It's not proper until after the wedding."

"But we're married," Riley said.

"Uh uh," Jing'er said. "Not until after the ceremony."

Both Riley and Dong held up their left hands with the matching red rings. The sparkles caught in the waning light.

"I don't care about the stardust ring," Jing'er said. "You should have a wedding."

"Stardust ring?" Riley looked at her hand, thumbing the ring. "That seems fitting."

"I guess," Jing'er said. Of course, she didn't know that Riley had felt the stars had moved at that moment.

"Riley said it felt like the very stars gave their blessing," Beatrice added.

Dong's voice was soft as he recited, "The stars wept when the Hidden One chose her beloved."

Riley looked at Dong. "What was it that you said?"

"He's been reading some celestial folklore," Jing'er said. "When he's had a chance that is. Do you want to know why he's been gone the past several days, all day, every day?"

Riley nodded. "Tell me."

"He got tricked into cleaning out the heavenly library for a month! A whole month."

"That's not important," Dong said. "But I learned something, and I think it is starting to make sense. Riley is what they call a Hidden One."

"I'm not familiar with that," Jing'er said.

Dong explained. "It's someone born of an immortal fae, who they themselves are not immortal. At least not in the way we think of immortals."

"Does that means I'm a fairy?" Riley asked. "What animal will I be able to turn into? Oh, I hope it's a fox." She skipped over to Dong, put her arms around him, and hopped up, giving him a quick kiss.

"Hello, Beautiful Wife," Dong greeted.

"Get a room," Jing'er cheerfully teased.

"How about it?" Dong said, wiggling his eyebrows.

"That would cause what that dolt thought Riley was," Beatrice said, frowning at Jing'er.

"Yes, ties that can not be undone," Jing'er said.

Dong looked over at his sister. "What did that dolt say about my woman?"

Riley turned red and said something very quietly. Too quietly for him to hear.

"He said what?" Dong asked again, gently.

Riley whispered into his ear. Dong shook his head.

"I told him it wasn't any of his business," Riley said. "Besides, we weren't even married a few months ago, so how could we be?" She smiled into his eyes. He had really nice eyes, especially when he was happy. She loved seeing him happy.

"Did you want kids?" Dong asked.

Riley blushed. "Someday. With you."

Dong's grin grew. "Really? With me? You know they would be half-foxes, they might be kind of furry and have sharp canines." He pointed to his teeth.

Riley pulled his hands away from his face.

Jing'er motioned for Beatrice to follow her to the stairs. "Let's let them talk. We can get Riley's belongings up to her room.

"I don't think she'll need her own room long," Beatrice said.

"Just a month," Jing'er said.

"Why do you say a month?"

Jing'er glanced back where Dong was leading Riley into the library.

"I don't think Dong will want to wait longer, and his gig cleaning the celestial library won't end for a month."

"You'll have to tell me how he got snagged into that." Beatrice shook her head.

Chapter 30

"Hey, Riley!" Lucas called. He jogged across the parking lot to the storefront, the late January snow turning to slush. "I wanted to apologize."

"There's no need," Riley said. She selected a grocery cart and pushed it along.

Lucas fell into step beside her. "I believe there is. I was out of line. It's just that I worry about you. Are you sure you know what you are doing?"

Riley nodded. "Very."

Lucas's next question came very quietly. "Do you know what he is?"

Riley stopped walking. She studied Lucas a moment. He couldn't possibly know what Dong was.

Riley resumed pushing her cart. She'd have to make this trip quick.

Lucas followed. "Riley."

Riley stopped at an open cart of apples. "He's a man who is very important to me."

"I have something I want to show you." Lucas reached out and took Riley's arm and a blast of bitter cold engulfed her. Suddenly, it was pitch black; the thick darkness that she felt was suffocating. Just as quickly, it ended. They were now in an open field. The sun was shining high in the sky. Here it was warm, balmy. Riley started to sweat under her winter coat.

Lucas spoke. "First, I need to tell you what I am. I am a wróżka."

"Isn't that your name? From Poland or something."

"Wróżka means fairy. It is also what I am. An immortal. Just as you are."

"I'm not a fairy," Riley said.

"You have magic in your blood." Lucas picked up her left hand. "This ring proves it."

Riley pulled her hand free. "My wedding band? It's just a ring."

Lucas shook his head, his brow furrowed. Was he angry?

Riley took a step back. "Why did you bring me here?"

Lucas stepped closer. "Can you answer my question, do you know *what* Dong is?"

"I don't see how that matters," Riley said, folding her arms across her chest. "Let's say I do. So what?"

"I will take that to mean yes. Follow me," Lucas said. He lead her a short distance to a little cottage. The door opened for him and he guided Riley inside. "You can take off your coat. After we talk, I'll take you back, or to wherever you want to go."

Riley took a seat but didn't move to take off her coat. She didn't want to stay there longer than she had to.

"We are friends," he said.

"Are we?" Riley asked.

"Riley, please. I'm trying to help you." He took off his coat and put it on a hook by the door. He held out his hand for Riley's. After a moment, and only because she was getting overheated, she took her coat off and handed it to him.

Lucas took a moment to look at her coat next to his. "They look good together. We would have—"

"Lucas, stop." Riley wanted to go home. She didn't have time for this.

Lucas lowered his head. "I know. It's just, I've been looking for you for so long. Now that I've found you, it's hard to believe that a shifter found you first. He's beguiled you."

Riley turned her attention to the window. "Why is it spring here?"

"The immortal lands have different seasons than the human realm. Some even remain a single season. Here, where my home is, it is always summer."

"I would miss the other seasons," Riley said. Christmas was also the season Dong finally admitted he loved her, so she had another reason to love winter.

Lucas beamed. "So you can see staying with me."

"That's not what I meant," Riley said. "I will remain true to Dong. He's my husband."

Lucas stood up, shaking his head. "No, he isn't, not yet. Maybe he won't ever be."

Riley frowned. How did she get it through this guy's thick skull? Well, the stardust ring couldn't be undone. Her kind would only love once. She didn't quite understand what a hidden one was yet. It was all quite new, after all. She had more questions than she had answers to. But one thing was certain. The stardust ring she had created, was a testament to that love. And it was for Dong, and Dong alone.

"What if we did that which can't be undone?" she asked.

Lucas knelt by her chair and took her hands into his. "I already told you."

She pulled her hands away and stuck them securely under her legs. "We did what can't be undone. He's my husband."

Lucas got up and paced to the window. "It doesn't matter. Like I said. There are other ways to handle an unwed pregnancy. You don't have to marry that shifter. If you want to keep the baby, that's fine. I'll take care of him with you." He turned to face her. "That shifter isn't a good guy.

He's killed people. They all have. They get their powers by killing their spouses on their wedding night. I don't want that to happen to you. Or your baby."

Riley laughed. "Dong would never harm me."

"So you admit it, you know he's a shifter? Then why are you still with him? Is it because of the baby?" He moved to touch her stomach and hesitated.

"I'm not pregnant," Riley said, swatting him away. "You're being an idiot. I'm afraid we can't remain friends."

"We are friends." He went to a small shelf and took up a book. He held it out to Riley. "This is a book about shifters. There are many kinds. They claim to be immortals. They beguile their prey. Nothing good happens."

"Well, you are wrong."

"Do you have a fae stone?" Lucas asked.

The change in topic startled Riley. "What's a fae stone?"

"It's a type of seer stone. If one is gifted to you, or someone in your bloodline, you can use it to see what something truly is. An immortal can even use it to see possible futures. A demon can not see anything from it. Shifters are the most cunning of demons, for they deny what they are. Demons can hide from the stone, but there is a way trick one to reveal what they are."

Riley's realized he must be referring to her monocle stone. "What if I did have such a stone?"

"You can use it to see Dong's true form, his true nature."

"I already know that though," Riley said. But a nagging thought chewed at the back of her mind. Dong had told her she didn't know what she was asking by choosing him.

That she didn't understand what he was. Was what Lucas said true? Was Dong a demon? If he was one, had she chosen wrong? She looked at the stardust ring. If she had, her heart would break. And what did that mean about her being one of the hidden ones? If she had fallen in love with someone she shouldn't have, was she destined to be alone? Well, she had been alone. She would survive, either way. And she knew that Dong wasn't evil, demon or not.

She squared her shoulders. "I'm listening. What do I need to do?"

Lucas beamed. "I knew you would see reason. Now, remember, you can't let him know you are going to reveal what he truly he. He can deceive you if you do."

Chapter 31

Riley was quiet when she returned to Fox Hill. She was so distracted by her thoughts that she burned herself making dinner. Dong used some of his life force and healed her, then scolded her for not paying attention to what she was doing. When the tears started to escape her eyes, he stopped and hugged her tight.

"I'm sorry," he said. "I don't want you getting hurt and it's really hard with being away all day. It's my fault."

"Only two weeks left to go," Riley said. "Did you get to talk to the empress about our wedding plans?"

Dong nodded, his face brightening. "I did. She and the emperor are honored by our request. Jing'er wants to sew your wedding gown."

Riley rested her head against his chest. "She asked me. I told her yes."

"No one does better embroidery than Jing'er. Not even the elves."

She pulled away enough to look up at him, chin on his chest. "Elves embroider? And here I thought they just helped prepare Christmas gifts."

Dong chuckled. "Silly girl. You're cute. To answer your question though, they do, and of all the fae and immortals, they are the best. Jing'er studied under them."

"So that's why she rivals them. I've seen her needlework. I would be honored to wear a dress she sews for me."

Dong took her face into his hands and brushed away the last of the tears with his thumbs. "Did you want to tell me what has you distracted today?"

She wanted to talk to Dong about it. But not then. Not there. "Can we go to your house? I mean your courtyard house. Just you and me."

"Of course. When did you want to leave?"

"Let's go now," Riley said. "What season will it be there?"

"Uh, winter. The seasons there generally match this world, but since it's in the mountains, winter tends to come early and last longer. Why?"

"I wanted to make sure I dress appropriately. So coat and gloves it is." Riley reluctantly moved out of his arm to go for her coat.

Dong nodded, following her.

"Does some of the fairy and immortal realms stay a single season?"

Dong thought a moment. "It is possible, but I've never seen it. There are worlds without number."

Dong held Riley's coat while she put her arms through the sleeves. He was a true gentleman. One for the ages. But then, he had had a long time to learn to be a gentleman. She reached into her pocket for her gloves. None in the first pocket ... only one in the other. Did she drop one of her gloves? She glanced at the floor. Nothing. She furrowed her brow.

"What is it," Dong asked.

"I misplaced one of my gloves."

"I'll get you a new pair," Dong said. "You don't need them right now. Now that we've both been to my old home, I can take us directly with less magical effort."

Dong drew the pattern in the air and they walked through together. There was no unbearable coldness. No thick darkness. Just peace and light. Riley thumbed the monocle in her pocket. It was so much different than the unbearable darkness she had felt with Lucas. Dong was what she knew him to be. She hadn't fallen in love with a demon. He may be a shifter according to Lucas, but he was her shifter. Who knew, maybe part of her heritage was also being a shifter. Dong was learning about the hidden ones, and he had promised to tell her what he learned. But, the going was slow because he did have to complete his word to clean the heavenly library. And Dong said there were unlimited books. Imagine that, unlimited books.

"Can we stay here tonight?" Riley asked as they stepped into the cozy room. The wedding décor had been removed, and a small heater was in the middle of the room, keeping it warm. When had Dong found the time to clean it up?

"If you would like. Is there any special reason?"

"No Jing'er, no Beatrice. Just the two of us," Riley said.

Dong nodded, took his jacket off, and undid his tie. He placed those on a clothes rack.

"Jing'er thought we might want these," he said, opening a drawer in a low dresser. He pulled out a light blue silk nightgown, and matching slippers. From another drawer, he pulled out a dark blue robe. "These are for you."

Riley accepted them. "Can you turn around so I can change?"

"I can do better than that." He waved his hand and her clothing changed. He watched as Riley held the skirt of the gown out, twirling around.

"I feel like Cinderella," she said, coming to a stop and smiling at him.

Dong walked over to the bed and sat down, patting the mattress. "Cinderella deserves to sleep."

Riley walked over to him. "You must mean Cinderfella needs his sleep."

"Cinder what?" Dong asked as she joined him on the bed. Again, like last time, he pulled the blanket over her, enveloping her in it alone. He laid next to her, still in a shirt and dress pants, his comforting arm around her.

"Cinder*fella.* It's a play on Cinderella being male. And with your cleaning every day..."

Dong gave her a gentle squeeze. "Ha ha, very funny."

She closed her eyes, enjoying his closeness. His breathing slowed. After a while, she said, "Dong?"

After a moment, Dong murmured he had heard her.

"Don't give up on me."

He pulled her closer. "I won't ever."

Riley closed her eyes. She'd plan what to do in the morning. She no longer trusted Lucas. She couldn't use her monocle on him because he knew she had it. Lucas seemed to be determined to get her to abandon Dong and go with him. That Lucas had hidden he was immortal, all the while knowing she was magical, even before she knew it herself, left a bad feeling in her gut. Dong had never lied about what he was. In fact, his first concern had been her safety.

In the morning, Dong had a bowl of nuts and berries for them to share. Riley helped herself to a few berries. She felt comfortable and safe here. Of course, Dong being there probably had a lot to do with it, if she was being totally honest with herself.

"I'd like to stay here today, if that's all right," Riley said.

Dong nodded. "Did you want me to ask Jing'er to show you around today?"

"No, that's okay. I'd like you to show me around later though."

Dong peeled a nut and offered it to Riley. "It's a deal. I wish I didn't have to leave you."

"It's only a few weeks more, then you'll never have to leave me. You may even get sick of me," Riley said.

"Get sick of you? Never. You're my unstoppable sunshine." He pulled her into his warm embrace.

"Unstoppable sunshine. I like that."

"Jing'er has made sure there is a dress for you for going out," Dong said, showing her where the dress robes were. "The attire here is not the same as in your world. You could say it's almost like stepping back in time, but with all the modern amenities you are used to."

Riley touched the fabric lightly. "It's beautiful. I need to thank Jing'er. She truly has thought of everything." There was also a navy blue cloak for going out.

After they finished eating breakfast and tidied up, Dong bid her farewell and left for the heavenly library.

So far he hadn't learned much other than her father had been an immortal, but exactly who he was had been struck out of any records. The only clue he has was a single letter, an F. Today he was hoping he could find out who Riley's mother was. He hoped to find the book that recorded Riley's early life.

Chapter 32

The small white dragon Kai bowed low before the Empress. The empress indicated he could rise. "There is no need to bow, little imugi."

Kai lifted his head. He spoke telepathically. *"I have come as you've asked,"* Kai said. *"How may I be of assistance?"*

The empress spoke. "I need you to swiftly go to the land of green hills, north of Sunrise. There you will find her, the phoenix's daughter."

Kai looked up. "Lord Fènghuáng's child is alive?"

The empress bowed her head. "She is yet but a mortal. You will know her by this pearl." From her robe, she took out a small beautiful pearl. "She is also the bride of my beloved fox, Dong. I fear the dragon lord will be causing trouble for them soon. It is not something that can be prevented forever."

Kai trembled. If the dragon lord broke free, it would spell disaster. Not all dragons were honorable beings, after all. Especially the cursed winged dragons.

"I pledge to help her and aide in any way."

The empress bowed. "I am pleased to hear that," she said.

Kai bowed lower, before blinking through time and space from the empresses' garden to the little mountain town, to perch on a tree to wait for a mortal girl to open the window.

Riley rummaged through the wardrobe, looking for the red wedding attire that had once been worn by Dong. She wanted to repair it. She'd had to repair a few things growing up, and while she could handle a needle, it wouldn't be anywhere near as beautiful as what Jing'er could do. She had minimal sewing skills. Asking Jing'er for help though meant that it wouldn't be her gift to her husband. She had less than a month to make it and then she and Dong would have their wedding.

Her heart warmed as she thought about setting up a home with her husband. She wasn't sure where she wanted to live more, here in this enchanted world, or at Fox Hill where she had first felt at home. What she did know, was that she wanted to be with Dong. He was her home.

Dong had said there was a village nearby, so she hoped she could get the needed thread and material she would need for her project. If she could use magic, she'd sew him an entirely new wedding attire. However, she couldn't. The best she might be able to manage was to mend it and hope Dong understood her heart. His past was what made him who he was, and she loved him in his entirety. To her, repairing his garment was the best way to show that. She examined the torn fabric, then the seams that held the outfit together. With a bit of luck, she could do this.

Getting up to stretch, Riley went to the window and opened it. On the tree outside was a rather large white bird—no, a small dragon. Its long serpentine body stretched out on the branch. Its dark eyes watched her curiously. He had a small white orb in his hand that glowed.

"Hello," Riley said. "Are you a dragon?" What a silly question, the only thing it could be was a dragon.

"I am," the dragon answered, his pearly orb vanishing. "Are you a phoenix?"

"A phoenix? No, I'm a human girl. I'm Riley."

The small dragon leaped off the tree and floated over to the window, landing on the sill.

"I only asked if you were a phoenix, Little Phoenix because you asked me if I was a dragon. I am, of course, a dragon."

"Oh, then I don't know if I am a phoenix. Dong tells me I am what is called a hidden one, and that means my father was an immortal."

The dragon nodded. "Fènghuáng, the first phoenix was your father."

"How do you know that? We've not met before."

"How do you know that we've not met? I may have met you before you could remember. On top of that, my gift is to see glimpses."

"I see," Riley said. "I've never met a dragon before. Aren't dragons usually big? You could probably sit on my shoulders, or I could hold you like a baby." She rocked an imaginary infant.

"I am not an infant, but I am a dragon," the dragon said, somewhat affronted. "I am called Kai."

"Do you want to come in?" she asked. "I have some nuts, berries, and water."

Kai launched off the window sill and flew into the room.

"Can you change shape?" Riley asked, fetching the bowl of berries for her guest.

"I cannot. I am just an imugi, not one of the higher dragons." Kai accepted the berries, using his hands to take one and eat. "I like you, Little Fènghuáng."

"You said that was my father's name. Fèng ... huáng."

Kai nodded. "The fox is seeking the knowledge, but it has been struck from the records to protect you when Fènghuáng and his wife died."

"I'm not sure I understand," Riley said. She wanted to ask so many questions that she couldn't think of a single one.

"The gods are mysterious in their ways. Your father was a high immortal, one of the gods. His brother was a dragon."

"How could my uncle be a dragon?"

Kai shook his head. "I didn't say *your* uncle was a dragon, I said your father's brother was a dragon." As if that made a difference.

"I don't understand," Riley said. "Isn't that the same thing?"

Kai ate another berry. "Yes, and no. Your father went to the mortal realm that year. The dragon did not. In your world, the dragon is not your uncle. But as a phoenix, he is. Yes?"

Riley sighed, handing the little dragon a nut. "Okay, I think I can follow that."

"Good," Kai said.

"Did you know my parents?" Riley asked.

Kai shook his head. "I did not. But I can tell you what I glimpsed. You are the daughter of the first phoenix. His blood is in your veins. To see the past, you will need to go to the tomb of the phoenix. Place the jade stone in the phoenix's eye as the last of the setting sun falls. For the present and the future, here is a wedding gift from me." Kai opened his palm and a small box appeared.

Riley thanked him, taking up the box. She set it on the table, where it grew to about the size of the average shoebox. "What in the world?"

"Open it," Kai said.

Riley lifted the lid off the box and carefully set it down. Inside, was a silvery spool of thread, a pair of scissors, and a needle carefully stuck into a thick fabric square.

"The scissors will cut what you need with no mistake, the thread will become what color you need, and the needle will guide your hand."

Underneath these things was a small miniature sized bolt of fabric. Riley carefully put it out. As she lifted it out of the box, it grew to a full-sized bolt of fabric.

"So you can make the wedding attire for your husband," Kai said. "I glimpsed what your heart desired. It is a good gift for your intended."

Riley brushed back tears. "Thank you." She scooped Kai up and hugged him. "Oh, I hope that was okay."

Kai straightened. "Because it was from you, yes. And you are welcome." The little dragon flew to the open window but turned back to Riley. "Be careful, little phoenix." Kai turned and launched himself in the air.

"Thank you, friend Kai," Riley called after him. "Please visit again. I can get more fruit and nuts for you."

In her mind, Riley felt Kai's response. Surprise, gratitude, and affection. She got a distinct impression that although the dragon hadn't known her long, he now viewed her as family.

Riley turned her attention to the fabric. She took Dong's old garment and looked carefully at the tear. The best way to repair it would be to cut the old off and sew in the new. The first step, she decided, was to deconstruct it to use it as a pattern. With great care, she worked out the stitches. Working steadily, she then cut the new fabric into the shapes she would need. By this time it was growing late. Dong would return soon with the falling of night. He would be hungry and she hadn't given a thought about dinner. She gathered up her project and packed it away in her magic box, which she put at the bottom of her wardrobe.

Riley didn't know what to do about dinner, so she decided to go exploring to see what she could find. Dong had left her a little purse of money, just in case she had need of anything. The cloak she wore was light, but just as Dong had promised, it was keeping her warm just as well as her coat would have, if not better, as it flowed to her ankles. She left from the front gate and started down the road. Dong had told her that his house was a bit outside of the village and it should only take about ten minutes to walk there. She tried not to dawdle as she saw what looked like a tiny dragon with butterfly wings stop by a delicate ice flower.

She smiled at the townspeople, who were out and about. She passed by an older woman who was sweeping her doorstep. She walked by a group of kids playing a game that involved tossing stones and trying to catch them on the back of their hands. A little boy was bouncing a ball along the cobblestone road.

The landscape was such that it seemed that the village was created and belonged in its mountain forest backdrop. Riley loved it. She felt more at home in this village than she did in the city where she had lived with Aunt Pat, or even the little town by Fox Hill.

A wider road ran through the center of the village. Sellers congregated there with their wares, as open-air structures kept them dry and out of the elements. There were fishmongers, sellers of fine goods like porcelain vases, and delicate decorative boxes. There were rings, hair combs, hairpins, and other jewelry. A tasseled pendant that would be worn at the waist caught her eye. The jade was carved into a fox with nine tales.

The hawker noticed her interest. "For you, that would be four bits of silver."

Not knowing if that was a fair price, Riley said, "Do you also have one with a phoenix?" While she liked the fox one, she thought Dong might prefer one of a phoenix. Especially once she told him she was one.

"I'm sorry, I don't. But, I do have a phoenix feather. Did you know that the phoenix is a legendary bird whose appearance is auspicious?"

"I didn't. Can I see the feather?" Riley asked.

"Of course," the old man said. He rummaged under his table and pulled out a cloth, carefully unwrapping it. A large red feather was indeed inside. When held up in the sunlight, it seemed to sparkle with red, blue, yellow, white, and black flecks of color. "It is very rare. A phoenix hasn't been seen for many, many years now."

Could this feather truly be a phoenix feather, she wondered. And if so, had it belonged to her father? Even if it didn't, she could use her mother's earrings and make Dong a decorative ornament for his waist.

"I'll take this and the fox jade," she said. "How much do I owe you?"

The hawker counted on his fingers and gave a number. Riley opened her purse and counted out the amount of silver requested. It looked like little stones. The old man counted them and seemed to weigh them in his hand. "Close enough."

"Thank you," Riley said. "Can you tell me a good place to eat?"

The old man pointed further down the road. "If you take a left there, there's a noodle and bun shop. I've heard they have the best in the village."

"Are you not from here?" Riley asked.

The old man shook his head. "Once a month many of us come here to sell our wares. We stay a few days, then head to the next village. This is our last day this week."

"Oh, I see." They were traveling merchants. "Thank you for the help," Riley said.

At the restaurant, Riley ordered two bowls of noodles and four steamed buns. She watched as the woman fetched the buns out of a tiered bamboo cooker. She accepted her goods and turned back towards home.

Chapter 33

Lucas trembled before the dragon, the great prince of darkness. His skin was dark as coal, his massive wings, dark as night. His claws were sharp and cruel

"My lord, I have found the phoenix," Lucas said.

"Why have you not brought her with you?" the dragon asked, tapping one of his sharp talons on the ground. Bits of dust jumped with each strike of his nail. "She has returned to the realm. Even I have felt it, the lingering

presence of my wretched foe."

Lucas tried not to watch the ground slowly get chipped away. He swallowed. "I have only just confirmed that she is the phoenix. I nearly had her, only that fox keeps getting in the way. He's bewitched her."

"Your task is to bring her to me. I am losing patience."

Lucas shook in his boots. "Yes, my lord."

The dragon paused in his stone chipping to study Lucas. "Have you developed feelings for her?"

Lucas's eyes flew wide. He did not want his adopted father to know this minute detail. That was why he hadn't brought Riley to him yet. If he could get Riley to be his wife beforehand, then surely his father would find another way. A way that would allow her to live.

"You have," the dragon said. "How interesting. You do realize her destiny lies with me?"

"You have only told me that you need her to unlock the chains that keep you here," Lucas said. He didn't need to say that all the other phoenixes he had found and brought there had died. He couldn't let that happen to Riley. He needed a way to circumvent her dying.

"It is good that you know. Her father locked me here, the daughter will release me. It is her duty. Yours is to bring her here."

Maybe if he got the dragon's promise, he could save her. "My lord, when I have completed my duty and she has completed hers, may I request she be given to me?"

"Oh?" The dragon stopped chipping away at the rocks and pointed his sharp deadly talon at Lucas's heart. "No one has ever dared to make a request from me. What makes you sure I will grant it?"

"Because once a dragon makes a promise, he is bound by it. I am bound to bring the phoenix here and I will bring her. That is if you promise that once her task is completed I can take her away from here."

The dragon chuckled. Rocks tumbled from the ground. "You would defy me for a woman?"

"For Riley, yes. While I am bound by the laws to complete the task I took upon me, Father, you lose nothing to give me one request. If you remember, I pledged to get you free when my birth father failed. I didn't pledge the manner I complete it. I will free you from your shackles."

The dragon growled and the walls trembled. "The phoenix is the only way."

"Promise me!"

The dragon's long mouth turned up in a smile, sharp teeth revealed. He lowered his large head to directly look into Lucas's eyes. "The woman will be yours. Now bring her here. Take some of my men to get her. Time is growing short."

"Yes, my lord." Lucas bowed, turned on his heel, and left.

The dragon watched him go. Yes, he could give the woman to him. Her phoenix essence would be gone. He needed the phoenix, he did not need the mortal woman. How fortunate it was for him that the phoenix was with a fox. And not just any fox, a favored nine-tailed fox of the empress. He would see the end to his two great enemies.

He hated the fox. They were the reason why he hadn't been able to free himself all those years ago. The foxes had aided the phoenix. They had spirited away the phoenix's child and hidden her. He would pay them back for it. He would take from the phoenix what was his, and destroy the fox tribe, starting with the fox that was by her side. Finally, he could right the wrongs against him. Revenge was good.

The dragon smiled. He would soon again be free. When he gained enough power, he would even overthrow the Emperor and Empress. This time, he would rule this realm.

Riley set a plate of the steamed buns next to Dong at the small table, before taking a seat next to him.

"Did you make these?" he asked.

"I went to the village today. I got the noodles and these there."

Dong took a bite of one and slowly chewed. "These are good, but I think you'd be able to make even better tasting steamed buns."

"You do?" Riley said. "I guess I should learn to make them."

Dong reached out and covered her hand with his. "Did you have a nice time in town?"

Riley's eyes lit up. "I did. But it took me longer than ten minutes to get there."

"It did? It usually takes me less than that."

"I'm sure it does because you aren't stopping along the way to look at all the amazing things. I saw what I thought was a butterfly, but when I looked closer, I realized it was a dragon with butterfly wings. Imagine that! I also saw a small fox with a unicorn horn." Riley pointed to her forehead. "So I thought maybe I would see a real unicorn among the trees, so I walked ever more slowly as I looked."

"Did you see one?" Dong asked.

"No, I didn't," she said with a pout.

"You're cute when you frown," Dong said.

Riley waved in protest, a delicate flush on her face. Dong made her feel pretty, even though it embarrassed her sometimes.

"You'll see more of the fae out as spring draws closer." Dong smiled and took another bite of the bun. After a moment, he spoke. "I learned a clue about your past. I found part of your genealogy records. Your father's name may have started with an F."

Riley nodded. "It does. That reminds me, I met Kai today."

"Kai?" Dong asked. "I am not familiar with Kai."

"He's a dragon, about so big." She indicated about the size of a parrot. "He has a serpentine body, two horns. He flew without wings. And he can talk.

"Kai can catch glimpses of the past, the present, or the future. He told me my father's name was Fènghuáng. He also told me I am a phoenix."

"You've learned more than I have been able to discover over a couple of weeks."

"We make a good team, you and I," Riley said.

"We do indeed." Dong smiled.

"Oh, I have something for you."

Dong was surprised. "You do?"

Riley took out the phoenix feather and handed it to Dong. She had added a beaded loop to it. "I'm told it is a phoenix feather."

Dong looked at it carefully. "Are these beads from your earrings?" he asked, touching the little beads of jade.

"It is. I wanted to give you something special, and I saw this vendor selling trinkets and ornaments. This one you wear at your waist."

"I know where to wear it. Are you sure you wish to give these to me?" He touched the little jade beads again, his eyes growing misty.

"Of course. This way you have a piece of me wherever you go. I mean, I can't guarantee that it truly is a phoenix feather. I have never seen one. But, my beads make it a part of me."

Dong leaned over, put his hand behind her head, and pulled her in for a kiss.

Once Riley was asleep, Dong sent a missive to Jing'er and Beatrice. He asked Jing'er to meet him at the celestial library, and for Beatrice to come and stay with Riley. With now knowing Riley's father's name and that she was a phoenix, Dong might be able to learn more. He needed to see the record of the phoenix tribe. Phoenixes were rare, and one of the smallest, if not the smallest, celestial tribe. It didn't make sense they would strike out the name of one of their own, which meant there had to be a reason. Add in the fact that he had seen Riley's ring fade gave him a sick feeling in his heart.

Chapter 34

R iley awoke to what sounded like bickering. Was she still dreaming?

"I'm here, you can leave!" Beatrice was saying, with a stomp to the ground.

"I am here, why don't you leave?" another voice said. It sounded vaguely familiar, yet she couldn't remember. Sitting up, Riley tried to brush the cobwebs from her brain. Gosh, was she tired. What time was it?

"What's going on so early?" Riley muttered. "Beatrice?"

Beatrice's face lit up and she leaned forward and stuck her tongue out at a little white dragon. "See, Riley is calling for me!"

"That is only because she heard your voice," the other voice said. Riley cleared the dust from her eyes and noticed the small white dragon, hands on his hips. If a dragon had hips.

"Oh, it's Kai," Riley said.

Beatrice spun to face Riley. "You know this rotten scoundrel?"

Riley nodded. "Beatrice, meet my new friend Kai. He's a dragon."

Beatrice frowned. "He's awful small for a dragon. Are you sure he's not just a lizard?" Beatrice stuck her tongue out at Kai.

"Yes, I am sure. Now be kind," Riley said. "Kai, this is my dear friend Beatrice. You'll have to excuse her. She is very protective of me."

Kai bowed. "Of course, little phoenix."

"Phoenix?" Beatrice said.

Riley smiled. "I am a bird fairy after all!"

"Oh my goodness. Riley, you are not just any bird-fairy then. You are one of the rarest. There hasn't been a phoenix seen in what, three hundred years? How are you a phoenix? Are you sure?"

"I have *seen it;* the empress has confirmed it. In fact, she sent me to help the phoenix," Kai said, folding his arms across his chest.

"She sent me to aid them first," Beatrice said. She turned her attention back to Riley. "Is that why Dong sent for us?"

"Us?" Riley asked.

Beatrice nodded, pacing as she talked. "This morning a letter arrived. He asked that Jing'er meet him at the celestial library and that I come here to stay with you."

"He didn't say anything to me," Riley said.

"Riley," Kai said. "Are we ready to head to your father's tomb? Is your husband coming with us?"

"Uh, I forgot to tell him that part," Riley said.

"I'm missing some information here," Beatrice said. "Start from the beginning."

Kai turned to Beatrice. "If I must. Here is a condensed version. Fènghuáng, the first phoenix, is Riley's father. She was born in the mortal world and hidden. But she has fallen in love with a fox and is now here, in this realm. To understand her past and to know where her future lays, she needs to go to her father's tomb and return the eye of the phoenix."

"What do you mean by return the eye to the phoenix?" Beatrice asked.

"I have to put the seer stone in the phoenix's eye, and I will see the past. I guess it's like a message my father left for me."

"Precisely," Kai said.

"How do we find the seer stone?"

"Do you think it might be my monocle stone?" Riley asked.

Beatrice threw up her arms. "How am I to know? Maybe?"

"It's worth a try. I have it here. " Riley went and retrieved a small box from the shelf and carefully took the monocle out. She set it to her eye and looked at Kai. "Yes, he is indeed a dragon. Just as expected."

"Can I see that?" Kai asked, holding out his hand.

Riley handed it to him, just as the door burst open.

Three masked men, in flowing black robes stood there, a large demon dog beside them. One of them had her lost mitten in his hands. They had their attention focused on Riley.

Kai grabbed hold of Riley and dove through the window. Another demon dog was sniffing the ground under it. It caught sight and scent of them and howled.

"Riley," Kai said urgently. "I can quickly carry us away from here. I think our best option is to go straight to the tomb. The dragon lord now knows you are here. Those are his minions."

Beatrice flew up, catching the last of Kai's words. "I will let Dong know where you are headed. We will follow as quickly as we can. Kai, keep Riley safe or I will peck your eyes out!"

Kai snorted, then disappeared into the sky with Riley. In a flash, they were gone. Beatrice looked down. The dogs were howling. The black robbed men were searching the grounds. They must be looking to see if Riley was hiding. Good thing Kai had carried her away. Why were they after her though?

Beatrice was certainly worried. Well, she needed to get to the celestial library post-haste. If only she travel faster.

Dong and Jing'er were quietly pouring over books and scrolls. The Lore Keeper brought over another pile.

"Don't you know what is in each record?" Jing'er asked.

The Lore Keeper frowned. "It is not for me to remember all things, only to watch over the library. I do, however, know that these books are pertinent to the phoenix."

"There's so many of them," Jing'er said.

"Keep looking, one of these should mention him and his life in mortality. It has to be recent. Riley is only eighteen," Dong said.

"I'm sure something is mentioned, somewhere," Jing'er said. "We will find—"

"Something bad has happened!!" Beatrice called as she flew into the library, a ball of sparkles.

A coldness gripped Dong's heart and he leapt up. "What has happened?"

"Kai took Riley," Beatrice said. "She is safe for now."

"Beatrice, slow down," Jing'er said. She put a hand on Dong's shoulder and he stilled. She nodded and Dong sat back down.

Beatrice took a seat and calmed her breathing.

"Speak," Dong said, impatience making him sound almost angry.

"As you had asked, I went over to hang out with Riley. Kai was already there and tried to insist I—"

"Get to the point," Jing'er said, noticing Dong's lack of patience. He was wound up tight, ready to spring out of the room.

Beatrice glanced at Dong, then focused her attention on the more calming expression of Jing'er. "Soldiers in black came, with their demon-hounds. Kai grabbed Riley and flew off, and I came here."

"Did Kai say where they were going?" Dong asked.

"To the tomb of the phoenix," Beatrice said.

"Why is there a tomb?" Jing'er looked at the Lore Keeper. "Don't phoenixes rise from the dead?"

"That is the lore," the Lore Keeper said. "But they can die. Every living being, in some form, must transcend one life to the next." He selected one of the books he had just given the foxes and opening it, set it in front of Dong. "The map to the tomb is here."

Dong looked at the book. "Nothing is marked on it," he said.

"Do you have the key?" the Lore keeper asked. "Not all that is written is as it appears. With the key, you will see where to go."

"What is this key? Where do I find it?" Dong asked.

"That I do not know," the Lore Keeper said.

Jing'er was silent for a while before her face lit up. "I think I got it!" She pushed aside the book she had been reading and opened up a wooden scroll. "This here mentions that together with the dragon prince, the phoenix king fashioned a jade ring that was key to— it stops here, it's been scratched out. But it has to be it."

"Is there any other mention of a jade ring?" Beatrice asked.

Jing'er shook her head. "Not that I've seen yet. Dong?" When he didn't answer after a moment, Jing'er called him again.

Dong blinked and looked at his waist ornament. Jade beads from Riley's earrings. Riley's box with her mother's handwriting on it. A jade stone, jade earrings, and a jade ring. "Riley."

"Riley what?" Beatrice said, flapping her arms in agitation.

"She's had it all along," Dong said. "Riley's mother left her a box. Inside were three objects. The first, a flat stone with a beaded chain. Second," he indicated his beads, "earrings. And third, a jade ring."

"She wasn't wearing a jade ring," Beatrice said.

"Dong, I'll go to Fox Hill to look for it, and you go to the cottage and look there. But be careful in case those hounds are still there."

Dong nodded.

"What am I to do?" Beatrice asked.

Dong looked at Beatrice. "I doubt Riley will return to the country house, having been chased out. Go to Fox Hill and wait for her in case she goes there."

Beatrice nodded and flew after Jing'er.

Dong hoped with all his heart that he could learn the location of the tomb and find Riley.

Chapter 35

Kai and Riley stood in front of an overgrown tomb. Riley walked over to it and started cleaning off weeds and dirt. A bird was carved into the stone. Riley ran her fingers over it, tracing the lines. The beak, the round eye like the sun, its strong back, the long feathers, and stork-like legs. "So this is the phoenix," she said. "Is this your final resting place, Dad?"

There was no answer.

Kai handed Riley the monocle. She studied it and looked back at the phoenix carving.

"I've always wanted to know where I came from. Why Aunt Pat was unkind to me. Now it seems I might be able to learn all of that here. It seems there is a bigger question out there now, too. Why am I being hunted?" She looked up at the sky. "Mom, Dad? If you are out there, can you help me? Somehow?"

A chilling dog howl split the air. It was so close.

"I don't think we have time to wait for Dong," Kai said. "Or the setting sun."

Riley nodded. Taking a deep breath, she set the monocle in the phoenixes' eye. And was suddenly caught up in a vision.

Memories, faint, enveloped her. Her father, cradling her in his arms, singing her to sleep. Her mother, dancing outside with her. Picking flowers together. A red fox in the yard, letting her pull on its tail—no, tails. A chilling wind. Thunder. Men in black robes, flowing in the wind. Her mother handing her to the fox, telling them to go. Swords. The fox fleeing with her. Huddling in the storm, in a warm woodsy den.

"My dear child," Fènghuáng said. "You have finally come."

Riley studied the man in front of her. He wore long robes of white with red trim, his hair long and dark. She recognized him. A longing filled her.

"Dad," she said, rushing forward. When her arms went to embrace him, she caught nothing but air. "What is this?" She turned back to look at the spirit before her.

"I have left a small part of my essence here," he said, as the image faded before returning in brightness. "I have waited many years for you."

Riley brushed back tears. "Where's Mom?"

Fènghuáng looked to his side, a tender smile gracing his face. "She is here, although what is left of my essence is not enough for you to see her. But she can see you. She loves you, Riley, very much."

Another howl, this time closer. "They are coming," Kai said.

"We haven't much time then," Fènghuáng said. "Daughter, you must listen carefully. Many years ago, I was one of the two immortals that bound the dark lord to his prison. To keep you safe, one of the empresses' celestial foxes took you and hid you. All mention of my bloodline was removed from the celestial records. It was as if I, and you by extension, had never lived. If you are here, I fear it means you are in danger."

"What do I do?" Riley asked.

"Love is the strongest magic. It can protect you. Phoenixes are beings that only love once, no matter how many times we may rise from the ashes. Some rise once, some many times."

Riley looked at her ring. "Dong—"

The hounds crashed through the brush.

"Riley, hurry! We have to go!" Kai yelled.

"Hold fast to love, Riley. That's the only way. The dragon cannot defeat love. Have hope." The image of her father faded as cold steel pressed on her neck.

"Now, finally we have you," Lucas said.

"Lucas?" Riley slowly turned, looking to where Lucas stood, watching the men cloaked in black.

Lucas stepped closer and spoke quietly, for her ears only. "I can help you, Riley. But you have to listen to me." He nodded to his men, barking an order. "Let's go."

Riley tried to spot Kai. Had he managed to get away and hide? The men seemed to be only focused on her, so she prayed that Kai was okay.

When they left, Kai, cloaked in an invisibility spell, slowly followed, being careful to avoid detection. He needed to know where they took Riley so he could bring the others.

Dong was at the country house, dismayed at the disarray. There was no sign of a struggle, but the rooms had been searched and torn apart. He started picking up items while he looked to see what was missing. He found Riley's box on the floor. It has been stepped on and damaged. Nothing was inside it. He set it on the dresser and picked up the clothes that has been thrown about. When he picked up Riley's robe, he heard a small tink as something hit the ground. It was the jade ring. He picked it up and closed his fingers around it. He would find Riley. He had to. He spun to the door as Jing'er entered the room.

"Did you find anything?" she asked.

He silently held out his hand, the jade ring on his palm.

"Let's go," Jing'er said, ready to rush back to the Celestial library.

"I have the map," Dong said. He carefully took the folded paper out of his sleeve.

"I thought nothing was allowed to leave the library," Jing'er said with a smile.

"Rules have been known to be broken," Dong said. "Besides, time is of the essence."

"I, for one, am proud of you brother," Jing'er said. She opened the map and placed it on the table. "What do we do now?"

Dong looked at the ring, then slipped it on his finger opposite the stardust ring. Then he held his hands, palm facing palm. A jade-green light grew between his hands, which he then focused on the map. When the ball of green light hit the paper, the map glowed. When it faded, the map was marked.

"The Tomb of the Phoenix," Jing'er whispered.

Dong nodded, and with a quick incantation, the two of them departed.

Riley glared at Lucas. She was tied to a pole. "Is this how you treat your friends?" Riley asked.

Lucas growled in frustration. "Friends? Didn't you tell me that we were no longer friends?"

"I was angry, Lucas. Why are you doing this?"

"I don't have a choice, Riley." Lucas said. "My father requires your assistance."

Riley scoffed. "Really? Then why didn't he ask me instead of forcing me to come by sword point?"

"You made it thus!" Lucas yelled. "If you had simply chosen me instead of that filthy fox, I could have brought you to meet Father. I could have convinced him to—"

Riley turned away.

"You can still pick me. You can still choose to help me free Father."

"I'm never going to choose you," Riley said. "And I certainly don't want him free."

A low rumble grew, rattling the stone walls. "So, you are the phoenix. Welcome to my humble abode," a man said. He wore black robes, that oddly shimmered. His hair was long and ink-black. His eyes were lined in black. His skin was flawless. He was breathtakingly beautiful.

"Father," Lucas said, bowing.

"You may leave, Lucas. I would talk with our guest."

Lucas glanced uneasily at Riley, then with his attention back on his father he said, "Of course." As he walked out of the room, the dragon spoke.

"You don't need those," he said. With a wave of his hand, the ropes tying Riley were loosened. "Forgive my adopted son his rudeness. He is young and impulsive."

Riley rubbed her wrist but said nothing as she weighed the situation. Based on what her father had said, she was sure this was the dark lord. But was he man or dragon? "Who are you?" she asked.

"I am he who has existed since the beginning of time," he said. "I am the bringer of life and death. I am the storm. I am Burza Smok, god of storms and darkness."

"I've never heard of you," Riley said.

Burza smiled. "Are you so sure of that, Riley? We've met before, years ago." Burza touched Riley's cheek gently with his hand. Riley went rigid, trying not to flinch with his cold, scaley touch. He was most definitely not a man, no matter what he looked like. She focused on that, while an image appeared in her mind. It was of her. She couldn't have been more than three. A knock at the door, and she opened it. A man stood there. He was beautiful. He knelt down and touched her cheek, just as he had now. Riley cried as her mother rushed over and scooped her up. Her mother stared at the man and told him to leave. As she moved to shut the door, a strong wind ripped it open, tearing it off its hinges. Riley's mother gave Riley to their pet fox and spoke quietly to the fox. The fox took off running. Thunder, loud and terrifying. The pounding of men running.

Riley trembled.

"You remember now, don't you? It took all my effort to project myself there, in the mortal world. Who would have thought that Fènghuáng had been hiding there, living as a mortal without his powers? His my mistake was my good fortune."

"What do you mean?" Riley asked.

"Had your father remained here in the spiritual realm, I would never have defeated the other immortal that imprisoned me. The seal would never have weakened enough for me to send forth my soul, and I would not have found Fènghuáng. Unfortunately, because he had a child, his death did nothing to break my chains."

"You'll stay imprisoned if I have anything to say about it."

Thunder rumbled, low and long.

"Are you so sure? I am a dragon god," Burza said. "I am not one of those gentle wishy-washy ones that only wish to bless the realms and those that inhabit it. No, I desire to rule it. I will crush those who oppose me. I will start with your world, with you at my side to stand witness, of course."

"Never," Riley said, holding her chin up in defiance.

Burza's nail became a claw, which he ran along Riley's cheek. "Ah, well, the choice is yours, of course. You can be at my side, or you will scatter to ashes." He picked up a lock of her long hair and looked into her eyes.

"I guess I die then," Riley said.

Burza chuckled. "It's not that simple, little phoenix. I need your essence to return my full powers and release me from my prison. There are two ways for me to receive it. One, you become my bride, thereby giving it to me. I could save your soul then. The other is, I drain it of you with your blood. If I drain it with your blood, your soul may shatter and scatter, never to be reborn."

"I'll take my chances," Riley said. "I've already chosen my husband. I'm married. I could never marry anyone else." She showed the dragon the stardust ring.

"Ah, so the phoenix has already chosen." Burza flicked his wrist, and Riley found herself secured back to the post. "It is too late then for the easy route then. It's a pity. You are the only heir to the phoenix tribe and the only one that can release their souls, locked in the abyss. I will ask again, Riley. Will you give yourself to me and hand me your stardust ring? I promise to release all the phoenixes. Even your father."

"You're mad," Riley said, trying to free herself. "Why would I marry someone like you?"

Burza smiled, and Riley noticed he had sharp pointed teeth. "As one of my women, I could have spared you, as I wouldn't need every last drop of your blood, as your growing love for me would have strengthened your essence. It would be infinite."

Riley laughed. "Love you? Don't make me sick."

Burza shrugged. "Love is a choice. If you chose me and the ring was then created for me, it would grant me the power of your essence as if I took your qi from you. I would then keep you for as long as you were useful."

"So I'd simply be a sickening snack forever?"

Burza nodded. "You catch on." He waved for one of his cloaked men to come forward. "Unfortunately, we have to go this route. I would have preferred the former, but this way works."

"What are you going to do?" Riley struggled, trying to loosen the ropes that tied her.

Burza pulled out what looked like a wooden straw. "Good. Keep fighting. The more your blood flows, and the stronger your will to survive, the more power in your life force." He tapped Riley's arm with his claw, then stabbed her, placing the straw into her vein. His blood-covered claw he studied, brought to his nose and inhaled, before putting it daintily in his mouth. "Very nice. There is great power here. You are indeed Fènghuáng's daughter." He nodded to his men. "Finish the job." Burza turned and left, leaving Riley alone with two guards. They stuck her arms with more of the grotesque wooden straws, letting her blood splatter slowly on the ground.

Was this truly how she died? Her father had told her to hold fast to love and not to give up. Well, she had held fast. She had refused Burza. How could love defeat him though? Maybe if she held on, and her last thoughts were on her husband, maybe her dying wish would be enough to prevent Burza from using her to free himself.

"Dong," she whispered. He must be her first and last thought. Love had to win.

Chapter 36

Kai was cursing. They had taken Riley to where the dark lord was imprisoned. He could not enter without alerting that vile beast to his presence. He needed to get back to the tomb, but he did not want to leave Riley alone, but did he really have a choice? The best chance to help her was to find Dong and the others.

When he got back to the tomb, he quickly noticed there were two people there. He decided to watch to see if they

were friend or foe. He couldn't make a mistake. Riley was depending on him.

"She's not here," Dong said as he searched the cemetery.

Jing'er studied a large stone. "She was here. Look." She pointed to where the flat stone was in the phoenixes' eye.

Dong looked around for any sign of a struggle.

"I don't smell any blood," Jing'er said. "I think Riley is okay for now. Don't worry, brother, we will find her."

Dong glanced at his ring, which caught the setting sunlight. "I hope you are right."

"Of course I am," Jing'er said.

Kai, realizing who they must be, interrupted them. "Are you Dong?" Kai asked.

Dong spun around. "I am. Who are you?"

Kai revealed himself, releasing his invisibility spell. "I am Kai."

Dong recognized the name, if not the dragon. Riley had told him about Kai.

"Where's Riley?" Jing'er asked, stepping closer. "Why isn't she with you?"

"She was taken to the dark lord's realm."

Dong turned to leave but stopped short. He didn't know how to get there. "Take me there," said, turning to look at Kai.

Kai bowed in acknowledgment.

"We might need this," Jing'er said, touching the stone in the phoenixes' eye. It sparkled and Fènghuáng appeared.

"Lord Fènghuáng," Kai said, bowing.

Dong and Jing'er looked at the image of the phoenix. Jing'er left the stone where it was.

"You are Riley's father?" Dong asked.

"I am," Fènghuáng said.

Dong bowed in respect.

Fènghuáng's eyes studied Dong, landing on the ring. "You are the one my daughter chose. Is your love true?"

Dong looked at his hand and gave a nod. "I love your daughter," he said. There was nothing else that needed to be said.

"Don't let her soul scatter," Fènghuáng said. "Save my daughter."

Dong nodded. "Can you help me get to the dark lord's lair?"

Fènghuáng was silent a moment. "I think I can, but I will need the help of all of you. And there is this— I can only send one."

"I'll go," Dong said.

"What? I want to help save Riley too," Jing'er said. "This time I can not stand by and do nothing while the woman my brother loves is in peril."

"Jing'er," Dong said, taking his sister's hands. "I should have told you this long ago. I don't hate you. I've never hated you for what happened before. I shouldn't have said it. I shouldn't have said I would never forgive you. I am sorry. I forgave you long ago. Will you forgive me?"

"Dong," Jing'er said, her voice breaking. "This isn't goodbye. Make it back with Riley."

Dong nodded, then turned back to Fènghuáng. "Okay, so what do we do?"

Riley woke up to the sound of droplets of water hitting the stone floor. She was cold, but she tried to focus on the sound of the water dripping. The sound proved she was yet alive. She felt like she had terrible stings all over her body. As she regained consciousness, she became more aware of her surroundings. She also realized the stings were those wooden needles she had been stabbed with. The droplets were her blood hitting the pavement. How much blood had she lost?

She struggled to keep her eyes open. Finally, she managed it. Her blood was filling up a shape carved in the floor. What was it of? She couldn't see enough of it, the red line of blood wasn't enough yet to reveal it all. That was a chilling thought.

"Dong will find me. I know it," she whispered to herself. "I'm not going to die here." She closed her heavy eyes, as memories danced behind her lids. The day she met Dong. His tearing up her lease. His face when she walked into his unlocked bathroom, the weight of his damp towel on her head. His cheeky expression when he had stomped dirt all over the house. How, when she fell off the ladder, his arms had kept her safe from harm. How he bent his head closer to her, before setting her down and scolding her. Her watching him, unbeknownst, practice his martial arts and swordsmanship in the evening setting sun. His comforting arms around her during a thunderstorm. Strange how she could even hear the distant thunder. Their raking leaves in the yard, and her showing him out to jump into the pile and toss leaves. A snowball fight when he took her to his real home. The wedding garb she meant to sew for him. She might not get to see him wear it, after all.

A tear streaked down her face.

The last thing Dong saw before he was transported away was his sister and Kai casting all their inner energy to Fènghuáng, who acted as a focal point to send Dong quickly to the lair of the dragon.

Fènghuáng had told him, by sharing his memories, that it was here that he and another god had bound Burza after he tried to conquer the mortal realm. He had brought war and destruction, and it had been all they could do to lock him in his home. Fènghuáng, who had just lost his wife and daughter, had been the one to reinforce the seal that locked him in place, giving up his chance to be reborn with it. With the forming of the seal, he had faded.

Now Dong understood why Fènghuáng's name has been removed from the celestial records. It was to protect Riley for as long as possible. Riley had also then been hidden in the mortal realm, the world of her mother. She hadn't been scared of him being a fox because of the spirit fox that had aided her all those many years ago. Dong would forever be grateful to that fox who had saved her.

And now, he would save Riley. There was no other option that was acceptable. He would reseal or kill the evil dragon, and save Riley.

His sister's words carried in the wind. "Kai and I will follow as soon as we can. Be safe, brother."

Chapter 37

Lucas was pacing outside the room where Riley was being kept. Surely he could convince her to give up on Dong and help his father. After all, all she needed to do was to break the seal that bound him. If she continued like this, she risked her very soul. The longer she was tortured, the higher the chance she would die when Burza took her magic.

Lucas knew that Riley wouldn't be allowed to leave this

realm once she unlocked the seal. Burza wouldn't allow it. She could not fall in the hands of the other immortals and reseal his adopted father. Surely though, he could provide a good life for them here. Certainly, she would come to realize this. Perhaps it would be better this way. In time, she would forget that fox. Eternity was a long time, after all. He could wait for her heart to be moved.

Lucas grimaced. He should have killed the fox when he first met him. Before Riley had married him. Great, he thought sarcastically, now he was thinking of her as being married to that vile fox. Well, that didn't matter. He still wanted Riley. His father had promised him she would be his. A phoenix and a dragon were well matched. They were destined to be a pair. Not that idiot Dong.

Not for the first time in his life, Lucas wished he hadn't been born a wyvern dragon. Long ago, the wyverns had chosen sides with Baal, the second eldest of the dragons, who had rebelled against the gods. It was because of this that Lucas had been raised by Burza, the eldest surviving son of Baal. But, if he hadn't been born a dragon, he would not have met Riley.

Could he have been different? Maybe if he'd been a fox, Riley would have chosen him. Of course, it did him no good to think that way. He couldn't help what he was born as, or how that meant he now had to watch as his father used Riley for his own purposes.

What was he going to do about Riley? He wanted to see her. No, he needed to see her, to make sure she was withstanding the life force removal process. He'd known

Riley wouldn't easily agree to break the seal. She didn't understand what was at stake for herself. Maybe he could still convince her. If his father got angry enough, he might kill Riley and they'd have to wait for her to be reborn before trying again to break the seal.

But, maybe that wasn't a bad thing. If she was reborn, he could find her before Dong did. If he was really lucky, his father would even kill Dong and save him the trouble of doing it himself. He didn't want the fox's blood on his hands. Foxes were sacred. He wasn't strong enough to go up against the empress. But once his father was free, he would be strong enough. And as the new crown prince of heaven, Lucas could have whatever woman he wanted.

Surely Dong would show up soon. Lucas knew that Dong loved Riley, just as he himself did. Dong wouldn't rest until he found her.

What if, the only way Dong could save her was to give her up? Lucas felt he knew the answer. That was the fox's weakness. He would put Riley before himself. When presented with the choice of her soul shattering forever in death or giving her up to save her, Dong would give her up. That Lucas was sure of.

Lucas would put his wants first. And he wanted Riley, even if he had to wait a dozen lifetimes for her. He was patient. In time, Riley would see that Lucas was right. That she was happier with him.

When Dong died, he would then take the stardust ring from his lifeless carcass, and Riley would be his. He'd prevent her soul from vanishing. The ring would unite them when she rose again from the dust. His father would help him. After all, he had promised he would give Riley to him. And once a dragon made a promise, he was bound by it. Even a demon dragon. Lucas decided he would be patient and wait.

Dong stood outside the dragon's lair. Somehow, Fenghuang had pulled it off. He'd opened a portal between realms. Dong looked at his remarkable stardust ring. It had glowed bright, and the stars had led Dong through the darkness, lighting his way. Now he stood at the front of what appeared to be a cave. A magical barrier blocked the entrance, but upon inspecting it, Dong realized he could slip through a crack in it. If this was a trap, he had no way of knowing, but even if it was, he knew he must go forward to rescue Riley. She would be waiting for him.

Chapter 38

Dong kept to the walls as he crept slowly forward, his trusty sword at his side. His exceptional hearing aided him as he quickly took out the guards. Thunder rumbled outside, echoing in the walls of the cavern. The stardust in his ring twinkled for his eyes only, guiding him towards Riley. Even though the ring guided him, he sensed it weakening. Riley was in danger. He needed to find her as quickly as possible.

Around another bend and he was at an apparent dead end. However, the stars that guided him went through what appeared to be a wall. It must be a hidden door. He felt along the edges, looking for the switch.

His ears twitched as he heard footfalls approaching. He turned to look. It was Lucas.

"I knew you'd come," Lucas said.

"Where's my wife?" Dong asked, pointing his sword at Lucas.

"Will you stop calling her that?" Lucas yelled. "She isn't married to you."

"Our union doesn't require your approval," Dong said. "Ours is tied by the red string of fate. And by choice."

"I don't believe in the red string of fate," Lucas said. "It's a folktale the immortals created that humans believe in."

Dong took note of Lucas's choice of words. So, Lucas wasn't human. That would explain why Jing'er hadn't been able to use seduction magic on him. It wasn't that he had a charm, it was that he was immune to it. That meant he was at least one of the fae. Just what was he? And why was he working for a demon-dragon like Burza?

"I can see you have many questions," Lucas said. "I will make a deal with you. I will take you to Riley. Help me save her."

Dong eyed him warily. Could he trust him?

"Put down your sword," Lucas said. "If you want to see Riley alive, that is."

Dong hesitated, then tossed his sword down. It was better to find Riley first, then he would figure out his next step in getting her out of there.

"Good, that wasn't too hard, was it?" Lucas said. He nodded into the darkness and a black-cloaked figure stepped forward, soundlessly, and picked up Dong's sword. Another appeared right next to Dong and took his arm. Dong took in the situation quickly. These guards didn't touch the ground and moved soundlessly. A biting chill radiated out from them.

"What are these?" he asked, indicating the two men that flanked him.

Lucas eyed the figures with distaste. "These creatures? They are the personal servants of Burza. It won't do any good to kill them. They will simply return to the abyss until summoned again."

"Take me to Riley," Dong said.

Lucas nodded. "Of course. Follow me."

The abyss men kept hold of Dong's arms and followed Lucas through the now opened door. The heavy wall closed behind them. They were in a large room. A stone seat stood along the far wall. He could barely make it out in the darkness. Lucas continued walking to the other side of the room.

Dong stepped on something wet and—with a sickening feeling realized it was Riley's blood. In growing horror, he looked at the floor. Her blood was filling up a large emblem carved into the stone. A phoenix in flight. He tried to free himself from the vice grips of the two abyss men holding him.

Lucas lifted a hand and tilted his head towards where someone was tied to a large pole, her arms held out like a scarecrow. Blood was slowly dripping from multiple rods of some sort stuck into her skin.

"Riley!" Dong called

"Remember the deal," Lucas said.

Dong growled low in his throat.

"Riley has refused to help my father."

Dong looked at Lucas. "Your father?"

Lucas kept his eyes on Riley. "As it happens, unless she gives up on your love, he can't take all her qi without killing her."

The chill emanating from the abyss guards was nothing to the cold that took hold of Dong's heart.

"I'm afraid she'll die unless you give her up." Lucas turned to face Dong. "Give her ring to me and I promise to save her. I will save her. "

Dong glanced at Riley and saw her slow and shallow breathing, the ring on her left hand growing faint. No. He couldn't let Riley die. But he also couldn't betray her and give her to Lucas.

"Dong... don't," Riley's whisper carried to Dong's ears. She moved ever so slightly, lifting her head to look up in their direction. A smile tugged at her mouth, but her fatigue hindered it. "I knew you'd come save me, Dong," she said.

Lucas frowned and punched Dong hard in the gut.

"Is that any way to treat our newest guest?" Burza's voice asked from the dark corner where the stone chair was.

Dong looked over as Burza stood up and walked over to them.

Lucas bowed. "Father."

Everything clicked into place. The demon dragon had a son. And it was Lucas. That was why Lucas was here working for the dark one. Not only that, but it made Lucas one of the gods—of the demons and creatures of the abyss, but still a god nonetheless.

"You must be the nine-tailed fox that bewitched this woman," Burza said. He touched Riley's shoulder. Despite how tired she was, she attempted to move away from his touch.

"He didn't bewitch me," Riley said. "It was I who chose him. And I will not let you break free of the seal. When I die here, I'll take my magic with me to the next life."

Burza laughed. "Is that so?"

Riley locked eyes with Dong. There was much she wanted to tell him. But, she was too weak, too tired. She tried to send all the love for him she felt through her eyes. His ring was twinkling, calling to her. The red string of fate still tied them. She knew she would find Dong again, and that gave her strength and courage.

Burza suddenly smiled. The blood in the carved phoenix was starting to glow. Riley's essence was almost completely spent. He had thought for a moment that it wouldn't be enough, but by seeing her lover, she had regained some power. Exactly how, Burza wasn't sure. Was it love? Was it hope? Whatever it was, it was working. He clasped his hands. It wouldn't be long now. The phoenix would die, her soul would shatter, and he'd finally be free.

The ring on Riley's hand sparkled in response to the way Dong's ring twinkled. They were beacons, calling to each other.

"Dong," Riley whispered. "Is it really you? I'm not dreaming, am I?"

Dong blinked back tears. "Yes, dearest wife, it is really me."

"I wish ... I wish you could hold me ..." Riley's voice faded.

Dong tried again to break free. As he struggled against the abyss men, his arms were going numb. His legs gave out, also going numb.

"You can't break free from the abyss eaters," Lucas said. "Every time you struggle, they slowly drain your strength, eating at you until you are too weak to do anything." Dong stilled. He needed to be strong.

"I can save her," Lucas said. "But I need you to work with me."

"Can I trust you?" Dong asked.

Lucas glanced at this father, who was eagerly watching the phoenix etched on the floor slowly glowing brighter. "Yes."

Dong wasn't sure, but he didn't have much choice, did he? He needed Lucas to call off the abyss guards that held him. He needed to get to Riley and get her out of there. Once he got her away, he could infuse some of his qi into her core. At least enough to get her to a celestial healer. There had to be a way.

"What do you need me to do?" Dong asked. His heart lurched as Riley went limp. Her breathing grew fainter.

"Give me the stardust ring," Lucas whispered.

Dong hesitated. That ring was created out of the love he and Riley shared. He didn't want to give that to anybody, much less Lucas. But, it was just a piece of jewelry, magic or not. It had led him to Riley. Now he needed to do whatever it took to get her out of there alive. And he couldn't do that unless he was freed. He needed Lucas to believe he trusted him.

"Release me and I'll give it to you," Dong said. "You can have the ring."

Lucas beamed. "You can't go back on your word," Lucas said.

"I won't. But Riley must live," Dong said. "If she dies, I will surely kill you."

Lucas snapped his fingers at the guards. "You are dismissed. Go back to the abyss."

The cloaked figures bowed and faded away. Dong checked his arms to make sure they worked. Satisfied, he looked at his ring and slid it off his finger. The ring wasn't what made Riley his. It was her heart. He held the ring out for Lucas.

Lucas snatched it.

Burza lifted his eyes to watch. A red string went from the ring Lucas was holding to Riley's ring. As Lucas walked towards Riley, the blood on the floor lit up even more. Two pieces of the same token. Two hearts. Burza suddenly realized the implications. Riley's power alone wasn't enough anymore because she had used it to make the pair of rings. In other words, she had gifted a small part of herself to Dong. That part of her magic was now in Lucas's hands, and Lucas wouldn't be expecting what was to come next.

"Lucas," Burza said. "My son. I fulfill my promise, the woman is yours."

"I can take her away from here?" Lucas asked, putting the ring on his finger. It fit, what luck.

Burza smiled. "Untie her. She is free to go."

Lucas rushed over to Riley. He pulled out one of the wooden straws. Blood rushed freely out of the wound. Lucas frowned, hesitating a little. Then he pulled another one out, and another.

"She's bleeding out," Dong yelled, rushing over. He pressed firmly against the wounds.

"Stop her bleeding," Lucas said. "I'll untie her."

They were so focused on Riley that by the time Dong noticed Burza's approach, it was too late to block him. He threw Dong off to the side like a rag doll, his long claws impaling Lucas from behind.

Lucas's face drained of blood as he looked down. "Father, why?"

"I said I would give you the woman, and I have," Burza said. "You can join her in the afterlife." Burza pulled out his claw as Lucas slumped to the ground. With no one left supporting Riley, she fell forward, hitting the ground.

Burza took the ring from Lucas's finger and crushed it into dust. Riley's ring vanished.

"No!" Dong yelled, getting up. He stumbled towards Burza.

That was when Kai and Jing'er burst through the door. Kai nodded to Jing'er, who rushed over to Riley's still form.

Kai sent a blast of magic at Burza, knocking him from behind.

"What?" Burza yelled, spinning around. A small blue bird dove at his eyes. Burza swatted the small bird with force. She landed on the ground with a sickening crunch, changing form as she was knocked unconscious.

The distraction was enough. Dong quickly called his sword to him and sliced Burza. A deadly battle ensued, between dragon and fox. Both held their ground, Dong's desire to save Riley fueling his power. Yet Burza was powerful and winning.

Riley roused enough to see Dong struggling. He had multiple wounds. Something her father said tickled her memory. Her love could save him. She knew what she would do. She would give Dong all of her power. A teardrop fell into her blood on the ground. Despite the ring being gone, the stardust still encircled her finger. It twinkled, spreading out from where the ring had been until it surrounded Dong.

Dong had no time to lose. He swung his magic-infused sword into a deadly strike. The phoenix emblem on the floor burst into a red flame, and Dong stood in victory. He dropped his sword and rushed to Riley's side.

Red sparkling lights were surrounding Riley. She was fading. Jing'er was crying. Kai keeled in sorrow.

"No," Dong said. He quickly sent a blast of his qi into Riley and prayed he wasn't too late.

Chapter 39

Dong stood underneath a tree, the bright moon reflecting off the water of the small lake. A small white dragon stood sentinel, watching from a tree branch.

Jing'er approached, carrying two lanterns. She handed one to him. "Are you ready to make a wish?"

Dong swallowed, giving an affirmative nod. He held up his finger and wrote in the air, then infused his words into the lantern. It was the same wish he had been making the

past several months and would continue to make. It was his wish for Riley. For her to regain her health and awaken. Stepping forward, he set his lantern to the water. Jing'er followed suit.

Kai dropped down from the tree onto Dong's shoulder. "Be of good cheer," Kai said. "A phoenix is destined to rise."

"I know," Dong said. "I will wait for however long it takes."

"Riley is a fighter," Jing'er said. "I'm sure she'll return to us soon."

Dong looked at his empty ring finger. "I miss her." His voice broke, and he wept, with Jing'er and Kai standing watch.

The seasons came and went. A hundred years passed, and it was summer once again. Dong's hair was now long and tied back with a ribbon. His long robes had a phoenix embroidered on them.

Dong stood in a field of flowers, lost in his memories. He remembered how he had returned to Fox Hill to find a young slip of a woman in his house. When he had torn her lease agreement she had gone to battle with him, refusing to leave. Over time, she wiggled deep into his heart.

He shook his head as he remembered how he had declared her cooking to be terrible and walked out of the dining room. He remembered kneading bread with her. Laughing together as she taught him how to roast marshmallows over a fire in the fireplace. How right she felt in his arms when he caught her falling from the ladder. Her hurt expression when he dumped her in her car and told her to leave. How happy he had been when she came back home.

A gentle breeze caressed him. A faint, familiar scent caught his attention. He spun around and glanced up. A girl in a soft green dress was standing in the field. The sun danced in her red-brown hair. Covering her face was a painted white fox mask. His heart rate spiked. Without thinking about it, his feet started carrying him towards the woman in the field of flowers.

She noticed his approach and waited.

He drew closer, lifting a hand to touch her mask, but drew back. Was she really here in front of him?

Seemingly impatient with him, she grabbed his hand and tugged him closer.

"Do you know what I am?" she asked.

Dong tried not to smile. "It seems to me that you are a fox."

"Mmm. I might be." She nodded. "But I'm a very special fox."

"How is that?" he asked.

"I have ..." She made a show of counting on her fingers. "Nine tails."

"What a coincidence," he said. "So do I."

The masked girl bounced up on her feet. "That's amazing."

"I guess," Dong said with a shrug. He turned to leave. She grabbed hold of his long sleeve. He stopped and she let go.

She looked down at her feet. "Actually, you'll never believe what I am."

"Try me," Dong said, a smile tugging at his lips. This time, he let it stay.

"Okay," she said. Carefully, she lifted the mask from her face. "I'm a phoenix."

"Amazing," Dong said, putting his arm around her waist and pulling her close. "It just so happens I'm married to a phoenix."

"Oh, so a fox and a phoenix got married?"

Dong nodded. "Indeed. And what a love story it is."

Riley smiled and wiped away tears. "I'm sorry it took me so long."

"You're here now," Dong said.

Riley nodded. "I missed you."

"Shh," Dong said.

"I'm serious," Riley said. "The whole time I was waiting to break out of my egg I kept—"

Dong silenced her with a kiss. When he finished, Riley smiled up at him. "I liked that. Kiss me again."

"Of course," Dong said.

Riley put her arms around him and welcomed the kiss. She was home where she belonged.

Who would have thought that she, an unwanted orphan, would find a family with a nine-tailed fox and his sister, a small white dragon, and a blue bird-fairy?

A happy songbird started singing as she flew over the flower field, letting anyone who cared to listen know, that the phoenix had returned to her fox, and all was well in the world again. Following her flight flew several phoenixes, having also risen from their slumber.

It wasn't too long from then that a celestial wedding was held. The bride was beautiful in her red gown, sewn and embroidered by a beaming nine-tailed fox.

The first bow was to heaven. The bride and groom bowed to the Celestial Empress and Emperor. The empress and emperor nodded in acknowledgment.

The second bow was to the parents. Riley smiled at her father, Fènghuáng, and her mother. (Who it turns out, wasn't simply a mortal, but that, dear reader, is a tale for another day.)

The third bow was to each other. As Riley and Dong stood up, a cheer went up. Riley wiped tears from her eyes as she gazed out at those who had come to witness their union. Her parents. The foxes and fairies. The many phoenixes that had been freed from the abyss when they had vanquished Burza and Lucas.

"Kiss the bride!" Kai yelled.

The empress laughed and nodded.

Dong and Riley turned towards each other, and Dong held her tight.

"Forever my wife," he said. As his lips found hers, the red string of fate grew bright, and the stardust ring returned to their fingers.

And to this day, they remain happily married, standing together through weal and woe.

The End.

Glossary

Chinese
Gēgē: older brother
Jiějiě: older sister
Xiǎo gū: your husband's sister (sister-in-law)

Polish
wróżka: fairy
burza: storm
smok: dragon

Acknowledgments

This book wouldn't be possible without the love and support of my family. Thank you.

I'd also like to thank my editing team for helping me as I pushed to grow as an author.

The cover art is by JV Arts.

Interior art of the fox by Leigh Cover Designs.

Interior art of the phoenix by Ced.

And lastly, thank you, dear reader, for the support.

About Author

Erica enjoys writing romantic fantasy and fairytales.

You can find her on the web at:
  http://ericalaurie.com

If you enjoyed this book, please consider leaving a review.

Also By Erica

Eun Na and the Phantom
Foxtails: A Paranormal Regency Romance
Evangeline
Chung Jo and the Sea Dragon
It Started with a Lie
One Thousand Winters

Made in the USA
Las Vegas, NV
29 November 2024

12890654R10152